UNSTABLE

The Amygdala Syndrome

JACK HUNT

DIRECT RESPONSE PUBLISHING

Also By Jack Hunt

The Renegades
The Renegades 2: Aftermath
The Renegades 3: Fortress
The Renegades 4: Colony
The Renegades 5: United
Mavericks: Hunters Moon
Killing Time
State of Panic
State of Shock
State of Decay
Defiant
Phobia
Anxiety
Strain
Blackout
Darkest Hour
Final Impact
And Many More…

Dedication

For my family.

Prologue

The crack of a gun startled them.

"Not to worry. It's only the zoo's emergency response team going through a drill," Ms. Mendes said. Nick Jackson groaned, shaking his head as a stream of Marfa High School students disembarked from dusty yellow school buses. They'd been stuck on them for the last three hours. Mendes called out names while several assistant teachers prodded them like cattle to line up as if they were kindergarten kids. Any second now he was expecting to hold the hand of the person beside him and get in one straight line. It was so demeaning. He was seventeen years of age, and more than capable of making good decisions. Besides, his father was a cop for God's sake. Oh, but no, none of that mattered. In their eyes they were adolescent idiots lacking the brain capacity to handle anything before the magical age of twenty. The large crowd of teens talked among themselves in the parking lot as they prepared for a long hot day at the El Paso Zoo. The field trip had been planned for months, and for months he'd begged his mother to let him sit this one out, but she wouldn't let him. *It will do you good. Maybe you can teach them a thing or two.* Yeah, as if anyone would listen, he'd replied. Nick wouldn't have minded but he'd visited the place countless times because his mother had worked there as a zookeeper, well, that was until they moved to Marfa after Will died.

Everything changed after that fateful night.

"Hey, you," a familiar female voice said. Nick turned in time to see a dark-haired beauty jog over to a cluster of girls, a mere spitting distance from him. Almond-shaped face, intense green eyes and a body to die for. Yep, she was the real deal! Callie Madison, now there was a reason to show up. Suddenly the day didn't seem too bad. She'd been on the second school bus. He'd had his eyes on her for years but never had the nerve to summon anything more than a nod, a smile or a croaky reply. His eyebrow shot up and his pulse sped up just a little as he soaked her in. She was wearing flats, tight jeans and a comfortable green V-neck top that brought out the color in her eyes.

"Not in a million years, kid!" There was only one person that called him kid, his best friend, Devan Jones. They'd known each other since moving to Marfa. His father, Emerick, ran the local radio station in town, and when he wasn't sitting behind a video screen playing Fortnite for marathon lengths of time, he was usually helping his father. Emerick Jones, now there was a guy with issues. Anyway, why he insisted on calling him kid was anyone's guess. He felt his solid arm wrap around his shoulders as they both looked on at the tanned beauty. "Ah, she's a goddess, isn't she? Alas, us mortals can only dream of bathing in her river of milk and honey." Devan was wearing an angry red shirt, khaki pants and Nikes. He raised his aviator glasses up over his trimmed Afro hair.

Trimmed? Nick thought, beginning to frown.

"What the heck happened to your hair?" Nick asked. He was so used to seeing him sporting something that resembled a spongy microphone, he could barely recognize him now.

Devan ran a hand over his head. "Yeah, I'm going for the Shemar Moore look, *Criminal Minds* style, you know? I figure all the ladies love that guy."

"Yeah, right." Nick chuckled shaking his head. "It might help if you put some deodorant on." Nick shook off Devan's arm.

He pulled a face, then sniffed his own pit. "What? I used Axe."

"When? Last month?"

"Hilarious."

Mendes told them to be quiet and follow her. "We have a big day ahead of us. I don't want anyone straying from the path. You hear me? That means you, Mr. Jones!" she said without looking at Devan.

He rolled his eyes as they sauntered towards the entrance. "You know, Ms. Mendes, Nick's mother used to work here, I'm sure he could—"

Nick batted him in the chest cutting him off. "Shut up, man."

"What?" He smirked. "She did."

"I'm very aware of that, Mr. Jones. Perhaps Mr. Jackson would like to join me at the front?" Mendes said casting a glance over her shoulder.

Nick grimaced. "I'll take a pass, thanks."

"That wasn't a question, Mr. Jones."

Devan brought a fist up to his mouth to stop himself from cracking up laughing while patting him on the back with the other hand. Nick elbowed Devan in the ribs and grumbled as he made his way up to the front of the line. As he passed by Callie she glanced at him and smiled. Nick coughed, flashed a smile and quickly jogged on.

For the next hour Ms. Mendes insisted that he give a rolling commentary on the various animals of America, Asia and Africa. It seemed that the tour guide that was meant to take them around had been called away to an incident elsewhere in the zoo, so he ended up wandering around the 35-acre facility answering some of the dumbest questions he'd ever heard. He knew most of the kids were asking them just to be assholes. Nick glared at Devan as they made their way into the area for the lions of Africa. Fortunately Ms. Mendes had taken off to find one of the students who'd got lost along the way so she'd left him in charge of giving the rest of the students the rundown on the great beasts. From behind the glass they watched as two lions prowled under the Texas heat. Every now and again the animals would charge the glass giving everyone a scare.

"… And so that's why there are only 30,000 lions left in Africa," Nick said.

"That's real thrilling, Jackson," Seth Owen said nodding with his arms crossed. "My life feels complete now." He chuckled, as did a couple of his buddies who fist pumped him. Owen was what Nick referred to as an all-around American kid. On the surface he embodied the clean-cut persona that any family would have been proud of but that was just a sham. In Nick's eyes he was a privileged jock, the kind of guy who thought women were impressed when he rolled up in his daddy's Beemer, or when he told them how much he drank on the weekend. Yep, he was a first-class douche bag but he had one thing going for him — his relationship. He had his arm wrapped around Callie's waist and any chance he got he would lean in and nibble on her neck. What she saw in him was unknown, and why she ever said yes to date that gorilla could only be summed up as one of the world's greatest mysteries.

Nick was about to wave them on to the next thrilling animal when Trisha Niles squinted and tapped the glass.

"Hey, uh, is that guy meant to be in there?"

Heads turned. Nick was all too familiar with the dress code at the zoo. He remembered the light brown uniform his mother wore, which reminded him of a national park ranger. The guy inside the enclosure wasn't wearing that. He was wearing a blue T-shirt, jeans, sunglasses, a white baseball hat and had a backpack on. The weight of the situation set in as they watched the odd man clamber over a wall and drop down into the inner sanctuary. The sound of his boots hitting the dirt got the attention of the three lions. Their heads whipped around and the large beasts ambled over to investigate their new guest.

The guy removed his sunglasses and tossed them to the ground alongside his backpack that he'd already removed. He began waving his arms like angel's wings and hollering at the top of his voice while walking towards them.

"Shit," Nick said looking around for a zookeeper. "Devan, hey, take my backpack," he said tossing it to him and hurrying out searching for assistance. When he spotted one and told her what was happening, she immediately got on the radio and he heard the woman say, "Yeah, it's the same guy who tried to get into the alligator enclosure."

What? he thought.

The guy had to have been on drugs or something. No one in their right mind would climb in there unless they had a death wish. The zookeeper headed over to the fenced area and tried to get the attention of the man but he wasn't listening. Nick heard over the radio that they were sending over a team with a tranquilizer gun for the animals. Within minutes officials were on the scene trying to do their best to communicate with the guy before he got mauled to death. While they tried to coax him out, the rest of the students made their way around and joined Nick. All anyone could do was look on in horror, as the large cats got closer.

In the distance a wail of sirens cut the tension.

The fire department had been called in because in the past they'd had someone else do this and they'd had to keep the animals back using water. Whether that was going to work this time was to be seen. The man continued to walk forward in an intimidating manner. He was in his early forties, slightly graying hair, thin and strangely familiar. Any attempt at communicating with him failed.

"Sir! Please. Come towards me!" an official said

beckoning him with a wave.

Then, in an instant, one of the lions charged at him and bit his arm. The guy screamed and whether it was his cry or the lion not liking the taste, it released him and trotted away. With blood now dripping from his arm and him clutching it in pain, they all expected the guy to turn and get the hell out of there but he didn't. No. He just stood there as if frozen by fear itself. Again, another attack occurred at lightning speed, this time coming from one of the other lions. This one knocked him to the ground, latched on to his leg and dragged him a few feet before releasing him.

Officials were yelling, trying to distract the beasts as a fire truck came roaring up and swerved close to the enclosure. Stern-looking individuals hopped out in heavy jackets and yellow hard hats and without even being told what to do, grabbed a hose and began dragging it over. Meanwhile one of the zookeepers was in position with a rifle ready to tranquilize the animals.

But it was too late.

A furious attack, this time by two of the lions, occurred with such brutality that even if they could have stopped them, the man would have bled to death. Ms. Mendes had returned by now, drawn back by one of the assistant teachers. She tried to get the students to turn away but they were mesmerized by what was going on. Even as the man squirmed and then staggered to his feet with flesh hanging from his bones, he continued forward, though this time it was as if he was the attacker.

He let out a loud cry.

A keeper fired the tranquilizer hitting one of the lions but failed to get the other two. They lunged at the man and within seconds tore him apart, leaving nothing but mutilated flesh inside torn clothing.

"All right, back to the buses. Let's go!" Mendes yelled waving her arms furiously.

Many of the girls wept, traumatized by the event, other kids talked among themselves but most were in shock, unable to say anything. How could something like that happen?

"This shit happens all the time," Seth said. "Seriously, there's videos on YouTube." He waved his finger around near his head. "The guy was probably jacked up on drugs or suicidal."

"Shut the hell up, Seth," Nick said.

"I'm just saying."

"Yeah, well don't."

He chuckled then sneered. "Got a problem, Jackson?"

Before things kicked off, one of the teachers intervened. It didn't take long to get them back on the buses. They left early that day, as did the rest of the park visitors after zoo officials shut down the park. It would take several days before more details would emerge but in the interim, everyone had questions. Who was the man? Why had he climbed into the enclosure? Why had he acted as if he wasn't scared of them?

The answer would be terrifying.

Chapter 1

Two days later

His marriage fell apart long before the nation did. The tip of the ballpoint pen hovered a few inches over the bottom of divorce papers as Police Chief Brody Jackson finished reading the legal jargon. Hesitation. Sadness. Disbelief. He shook his head, unable to bring himself to sign it. Twenty-four years of marriage down the drain was a tough pill to swallow. He'd known the stats heading into his career in law enforcement, he just didn't think he'd become one. It wasn't meant to end like this. They were meant to grow old together. Images of them from better times replayed in his mind. Where had it all gone so wrong? He could claim ignorance but he knew why, well, at least he'd heard the third marriage counselor's palatable version once she'd listened to both sides.

And there were always two sides.

He hadn't cheated. He wasn't a drinker. And he

certainly wasn't a man prone to violent outbursts. He had a reputation in town to uphold and a career that relied on having a good head on his shoulders. Common sense guided him. But that didn't mean he wasn't without fault, he was human after all.

No, Brody was all too willing to admit his shortcomings. His wife? He wasn't sure. Any mention of her track record was seen as nothing more than an accusation, a means of deflecting from his baggage. But that wasn't the case, and he was too damn tired to argue. More often than not he would let it slide, retreat inward and do the one thing that kept his mind occupied — work.

Maybe that was the problem. It had been for many others.

The long shifts could be hard.

Being an officer wasn't a job, it was a career, a calling some would say.

He didn't clock out at five and drive home worry free. His mind was constantly swirling between office politics, unfinished investigations and the unfortunate horrors that tried to torment his mind.

It was now Friday, the middle of June, and the temperatures were hovering in the high eighties. It was going to be another hot and muggy day and since the air in his truck had given up the ghost and the shop couldn't fix it for another day, he was left to endure the heat.

The radio crackled. He heard Linda, the dispatcher, speaking with Officer Matt Niles. Brody reached for his morning cup of joe and contemplated calling Jenna and asking for more time. Maybe he'd overlooked something, perhaps she was being too hasty, and maybe it could all be solved with a long vacation away. Couldn't it? She didn't think so. No, in her mind it was too late for that. She'd made that perfectly clear when she took off, took out money from the account and distanced herself. The fire that had once burned so hot between them had died to nothing more than embers and lies, and no amount of talking was going to revive it. Conversations turned to arguments in the blink of an eye. "Communication is key," the counselor had said. No surprise there, that's what they'd drilled into them at the academy. After all these years he'd considered himself an expert in talking people down from the ledge but now he was at a loss for words. If talking it out could have resolved it, she wouldn't be living with her parents. He'd considered moving out so she could return but he was all too familiar with how the courts would label that — they would have said he abandoned his family — and he hadn't. He'd fought to prevent it falling apart. Hell, for the past six months it had been an exhausting battle.

Sitting behind the wheel, Brody rested an elbow on the door of his black 4 x 4 truck, lifted his hat and wiped a bead of sweat from his brow. He caught his reflection in the side mirror. At forty-five he was beginning to show his age. There were a few more lines at the corners of his eyes, and some strands of gray streaking his black hair. Brody ran a hand over his clean-shaven jaw and gazed out across the barren Chihuahuan desert of West Texas just on the outskirts of Marfa. The small town with just over two thousand people had been home for the past four years. He'd grown up in Alpine, a neighboring town, thirty minutes to the east. It was similar but different in many ways. Marfa was an oddball town full of hipsters and artists, in the middle of nowhere, literally. It was situated between the Davis Mountains and Big Bend National Park, three hours from the nearest airport in El Paso, and a good twenty miles from surrounding towns. It wasn't exactly a hub of activity except for on the weekends. Tourists, artists and commuters passed through, but occasionally it was those who were lost. Back when he was working with the Presidio County Sheriff's Office, he'd considered taking a position with Alpine's department but turned it down once the City of Marfa decided to cut ties with the county after using their law enforcement services for ten years. Fortunately, as fate would have it, Marfa officials decided to form their own police department and he'd been given the first kick at the can of being the chief. Now, there was him and four officers, and in some ways he liked that. It felt like a tight-knit family.

Brody breathed in the humid air.

He'd parked out by Marfa Viewing Area, just off US-90. It was a famous observation point for taking in the mysterious Marfa Lights, an unexplained phenomenon that had put Marfa on the map. Hell, they'd even added to the badge on his arm the words: Home of the mystery lights. He exhaled hard and gazed out. The sandstone, cylindrical adobe structure was a relic that once held good memories — shared ones. Now it only made him feel empty. He sighed again and tossed the divorce papers on the passenger seat and took another swig of his coffee. *Screw it. It can wait. Twenty-four years is a long time, another day won't hurt.*

His thoughts shifted to the missing woman, the reason he was there.

It had been five days since the college student had gone missing, and they were no further ahead in finding her. A few tips had come in but they hadn't panned out. In fact, diving into her history had produced almost nothing.

No ATM withdrawals. No cell phone activity. No posts on social media.

In today's modern age that was unheard of.

The situation was dire, that was for sure, and he wasn't holding out hope. His gut told him she was probably buried out there in the desolate desert beneath the Chinati Mountains. It would have been easy for anyone to drive out and dump a body in a shallow grave and no one would be the wiser. Few people ventured out there, and ranchers generally only had cameras set up to overlook livestock, not miles of desert.

Viola Ricci, twenty-one, hadn't shown up for class at Sul Ross State University on Monday. Although she'd been studying in the neighboring town, her family was from Marfa. They were good people, hard-working, the kind of folk that would have given you the shirt off their backs. Her father Martin Ricci had been assisting where he could and many of the students and residents had rallied together to form search teams that would comb the

Mitchell Flat and the vast region around both towns. Meanwhile Brody had been working closely with Alpine Police as they conducted interviews with friends, family and a former boyfriend because she had simply disappeared into thin air. They had already gone through every scenario. Was she under stress at college? Had she spoken about wanting to harm herself or run away? Did any of her friends notice her mood change? Were there any recent changes in her relationship with her ex? There was no connection they could make, though Marfa and Alpine were currently scrutinizing the ex-boyfriend.

That was what he'd been doing that morning, speaking with the chief of Alpine as a lead had come in from a young couple who had been out at the observation area hoping to see the lights. They said they saw a truck out near the base of the mountains. They wouldn't have been the first. It was common to see glowing lights in the air and on the ground, and because distance was a hard thing to judge, it would have been easy to mistake the lights for a vehicle.

An officer from Alpine and the young couple were meant to meet him there. As he waited, he glanced at the clock. It was nearly the top of the hour so he turned on the radio and tuned into Marfa Public Radio to catch the latest town news. Emerick Jones' voice came blasting out like a foghorn.

"... And that tune goes out to Sandra Andrews from her grandson. Have a wonderful day from all of us at here at the station. Now on to the news. Okay, folks, while I don't like to be a buzz kill, I've got to share some sad news about a good friend of mine — Bob Lincoln. While you might not recognize the name, you would probably recognize his face if you were one of the many people that bought a vehicle at Fitzgerald Auto Sales. It's with great sadness that I have to let you know that he passed away. Anyone who has been watching or reading the news will be aware of the animal attack at El Paso Zoo. Now of course, we don't like to speculate and we must be sensitive to the family at this time, but his son Jason reached out to us to make it clear that his father was a good man who had no history with drinking or drugs, so any rumors that say otherwise should be disregarded. I can certainly account for Bob myself. He was a straight and narrow kind of guy, a churchgoer, the kind of man that knew the value of family above all things. Anyway, his funeral will be held this afternoon at the Alpine Memorial Funeral Home. It's a private funeral for family only. So from us here at Marfa Public Radio, Jason and family, you are in our prayers and thoughts. And Bob, Godspeed."

Nick had told him about the incident. He couldn't believe it himself. The few times he'd met Bob, he too saw him as someone with a good head on his shoulders. He didn't strike him as a man with mental issues either.

Brody glanced out and saw a police cruiser pull in, kicking up dust. He switched off the radio and hopped out, removed his hat and wiped sweat from his brow. When the officer got out, Brody smirked.

"Officer Ray Gottman."

He gave a half-assed salute. "Chief."

The two of them went way back. Both had attended academy together and worked for the county before taking their respective positions in different towns. It had been a while since they'd seen each other, though Brody knew he was working for Alpine. Ray made his way over, briefly glancing back at the couple in the rear of his cruiser. There was another officer in the passenger side.

"Just a quick word before we get started."

"Sure," Brody said leaning against his truck. Ray eyed it and smiled. "Nice ride. Did the department pay for that?"

"No, last month's lottery ticket did," he said with a grin. "But don't be jealous, the air conditioning packed it in a couple of days ago. Anyway, what have we got?"

"They're a little skittish to talk. It took us a while just to get what we did out of them. They think they can pinpoint the location of where they saw the vehicle's headlights, but they don't want anyone to know they've helped. Oh, and they don't want to rehash what they were doing out there."

"I think that's self-explanatory."

While many came out to observe the lights, it was also a common spot for young couples to park their cars and get all hot and heavy. Gottman jerked his head towards the cruiser and the other officer let the couple out. The couple couldn't have been more than twenty. College material, wet behind the ears and scared by the looks of it. The guy had a dark mustache, and stubble. He was wearing flip flops, jeans and a lettered green T-shirt, and his girlfriend looked like she was on her way to Burning Man or Woodstock. She had dark hair in braids, with a flowery cut blouse and hip-hugging jeans with bell bottoms.

"Mike, Cecilia, this is Chief Brody Jackson."

"Hey, how are you?" Brody said extending a hand and attempting to put them at ease. It wasn't easy for witnesses to agree to come forward. Far too often the threat of retribution for saying anything kept lips sealed.

Mike nodded hard but said nothing. Cecilia stuck her hands in her back pockets and looked around nervously.

"How about you take me back to that night and what you saw? Can you do that?"

Mike nodded and made a gesture to the structure.

* * *

Colonel Nichol Lynch put the phone down and squeezed the bridge of her nose. She got up from her desk and went into the adjoining washroom and splashed some cold water over her face. As it dripped off her chin she stared into the small mirror and ran a hand over it. She couldn't believe it had happened. After working for the United States Army Medical Research Institute of Infectious Diseases (USAMRIID) at Fort Detrick for the better part of nine years, she was used to being called in to investigate outbreaks. Lynch was familiar with pandemic viruses being released into the population via "mock-up" vaccines by the World Health Organization in an attempt to get ahead of a real pandemic, but this was nothing like that. This wasn't a pandemic, it was a screw-up of epic proportion and as usual they had dumped it on her lap and she was left to handle the muck. She dried her face with a brown paper towel and tossed it in the garbage before coming out and pouring her second cup of coffee.

While the El Paso Zoo incident was considered the first known public case, it wasn't the first time they had dealt with this, the difference was the military said it was quarantined and the batch that caused the death of nine soldiers had been destroyed.

They said it was no longer a threat.

It was meant to have ended there. Obviously not, otherwise she wouldn't be missing out on her upcoming weekend getaway with her husband. She'd booked it well in advance; months ago after Wes had been voicing his concerns about the state of their relationship. She'd been struggling to keep the spark alive in their flailing marriage with increased workload and heavy demands. Her long hours and her constant trips around and outside of the country had eventually started to take their toll. This weekend was meant to fix that, or at least put a Band-Aid over the issue for another six months. She took a hard sip on her coffee and glanced at the photo of her husband. It probably wasn't good getting married to someone who wasn't in the military. They really couldn't understand the demands that were put on her or the lives that hung in the balance if she didn't do her job right. It was tough but rewarding in so many ways. She'd lost track of all the lives she'd saved, and the number of times the general public had narrowly avoided deadly outbreaks because of her.

Still, she was going to have to make the call.

"Damn it!" she said, spilling some coffee as she returned to her desk. *Can this day get any worse?*

It was what she was not being told about the incidents that worried her. She was used to protocol and having information shared to her on a need-to-know basis but in all her years investigating pandemics, she hadn't seen anything like this.

Of course she poked and probed for more details but what was shared was vague at best. From what she could piece together, the Pentagon had been working on a new form of drug to control fear and anxiety. Essentially an attempt to make fearless soldiers.

She'd heard through the grapevine that the United States Department of Defense had been working with a third-party biotechnology lab to develop advanced forms of bioelectrical medicines that could suppress fear in soldiers so that the chances of success on missions would be higher. But she didn't buy it, well, that was until she heard about DARPA getting involved and putting out an open challenge for labs to come up with a drug that might control fear and anxiety.

When asked why they were doing that, the DARPA official who had brought her up to speed on the incident had said that it was meant to be the answer for post-traumatic stress and to cut down on the high number of deaths of American soldiers.

It would regulate adrenaline, target the amygdala in the brain and produce a new kind of soldier, he'd said.

Yeah, right, she'd thought.

It certainly sounded like a palatable sound bite and she was sure the labs would have swallowed it down with great interest, especially since the Pentagon would be the ones footing the bill. But she knew the truth. It was all just smoke and mirrors for the real project, an undisclosed reason that only those higher up would be privy to.

She made the call to Wes and bit down on her lower lip expecting the worst.

"Hey, hon, so I packed the bags so we should be ready to…"

"Yeah about that, Wes," Lynch said.

He groaned. "Why don't I like the sound of that?"

She breathed in deeply. "Something's come up."

Lynch heard Wes sigh. "Typical. Please tell me it's just for today."

"Well that's the thing. I'm not exactly sure how long I'm going to be working on this."

Click.

The line went dead.

She closed her eyes and put a hand over her face. She knew he was going to lose his cool. She couldn't blame him. Lynch was as pissed as he was but she didn't have the type of job where she could tell them where to go. Some days she wished she'd stayed at a lower rank. But everyone said shit rolled downhill so she thought it would be better at the top. Nope.

She tried to call home again but he wouldn't answer.

That meant a week or two of silent treatment.

Lynch put the phone down and swigged her coffee. She shook the mouse beside her computer and the screen blinked to life. Next, she navigated to her email to see if the details of the El Paso Zoo case had arrived yet. *Nothing.*

Her orders so far were to focus in on some small town in the armpit of Texas, some desert shithole where the kids were from. Her job was to make sure that it didn't spread.

Easier said than done.

The media had already run a piece on the guy. She did a quick search for his name online and up came multiple listings showing the brutal video of the man being torn apart by lions. *Sick,* she thought.

On top of all of that, she would need to deal with the authorities in Marfa and that often was the worst part of the job. Especially if she was dealing with a cop or mayor with a chip on their shoulder. Many of them didn't like to take orders from anyone outside of their town, and even more so if it was a woman.

She hit pause when someone knocked at her door.

"Come in."

The door partly opened and Major Tim Brown stuck his head in. "You wanted to see me?"

"Yes, come in, Tim."

He entered and closed the door behind him.

She glanced down and saw the email come in with the report.

"I hope you are ready to hit the road. I'll send over the details to you. I would like to make sure that we keep this as quiet as possible. The last thing we need is the police breathing down our necks."

"That may be unavoidable."

Her brow furrowed. "Did you get the same email?"

"I received it earlier today. Fortunately it may be an isolated case. From what we can tell he was alone that day at the zoo and surveillance footage had him avoiding crowds."

Lynch nodded while she zigzagged the updated report hoping it would give her further details on the virus itself. Nope. Just details about how fast it spread within the group of soldiers. Their job was to investigate the town, isolate any further incidents and make sure the students who were the closest to the victim were checked.

Chapter 2

Jenna Jackson finished bandaging up the woman's hand. She was two hours over her scheduled eight-hour shift at Big Bend Regional Medical Center in Alpine. After years of working for the El Paso Zoo and losing their son Will in a car crash, they'd made the decision to start afresh somewhere else, so Brody took a job with the county and she went back to college to get her nursing diploma. Her mother had been a nurse and from an early age she'd always admired the career but was never sure if it was something she could do.

With Alpine being the closest major hospital for Marfa, and her marriage falling apart, she made the decision to move in with her parents in Alpine just until they'd finalized the divorce.

"Do you mind if I have a word with you privately?" Jenna asked the husband who had brought in the patient. Both were middle-aged, no older than fifty. There was something about the situation that didn't sit well with her. She came to learn the husband was a local preschool teacher and the woman a psychologist. She was known in these parts for helping both the police and locals manage their personal issues. That's why it struck Jenna as odd.

Outside the room, she glanced at Deidra Hamilton through the window. Martin closed the door behind him and turned to her. "Yes?"

"Martin, you said you found her with her hand on the stove?"

He nodded. "That's right."

"Is she on any medication?"

"None that I know."

"Alcohol?"

"She doesn't drink."

"Any mental health issues we should be aware of?"

He frowned. "Of course not. If she did she wouldn't be able to function in the community as a psychologist. The people who come to her are the ones with real problems. She fixes them."

"And you've never witnessed this kind of behavior before? No self-harm? Cutting? Attempts at taking her life?"

"None."

Jenna nodded and looked through the window. Deidra was staring at her bandaged hand and looked confused. The poor woman looked as if she was in some kind of comatose state. She responded to pain and commands like put your hand out, and overall there was nothing that would lead Jenna to believe that she was mentally unstable, but it was the circumstances of how she came to experience second-degree burns that concerned her most.

"So run it by me again. You walked in on her just as she placed her hand against the stove burner?"

"That's right. Yeah." He nodded, tears welling up in his eyes. "I pulled her away and she seemed confused but at the same time wildly curious about what would happen if she did it. I don't understand. What would make her do that?"

Jenna looked back at Deidra. "Well, Martin, that's

what we have to figure out. We're going to do some blood work, maybe run her through an MRI machine and see what it shows us." She looked back at him. "Are you sure there is nothing you can pinpoint? A moment when she started acting strange and out of sorts?"

He shook his head.

"And what about yourself? Are you okay?"

"Beyond being traumatized? Yeah," he said, a tear streaking his cheek. Jenna placed both hands on his arms.

"Hang tight, the doctor should be in shortly."

Martin headed back into the room to be with his wife while Jenna took her clipboard over to the center desk. Tina, a good friend and co-worker of hers, was busy juggling paperwork and speaking on the phone. She glanced at her and stuck the phone into the crook of her neck to indicate that she needed to talk. They had been rushed off their feet from the moment she started her shift. On any given day or night they could find themselves dealing with all manner of trauma victims, and trying to prioritize. Of course this often led to dealing with angry visitors who demanded to be seen immediately. Tina put the phone down. She spun in her seat and exhaled hard, running a hand around the back of her neck. She had a blond ponytail and was wearing blue scrubs.

"I need to take my break."

"Tina. We're overloaded right now. Can you hold off?"

"I was meant to take my break two hours ago. If I sit here any longer I'm going to pee myself and die of starvation."

Jenna laughed. "All right. I'll let them know where you've gone."

She wasn't in charge, per se, but Tina was new to the crew and Jenna had been given the task of making sure she was up to speed on how they operated and where they kept all the supplies. Tina darted out before anyone could change their mind, leaving Jenna to deal with an impatient man who was tapping his fingers against the counter.

"What does a person have to do to get a little help around here?" he asked.

"How can I help you?" she asked.

"We've been sitting in the blue, non-emergency ward for over two hours and no one has been by to see us."

"Sir, I can appreciate that. We usually try to get around to everyone within a four-hour window but it depends on how many patients have been admitted. Those with critical injuries are obviously going to be seen first, but be reassured we will get to you. Can I get your name?"

"Roger Whittaker."

She brought up the file. "Yeah, the doctor has you on his rounds. There are three people before you."

He scoffed and said, "What a joke this place is. And to think my tax dollars pay for this. I've seen better treatment in third world countries." With that said he returned to the small waiting room. Jenna understood people didn't like to wait and if she had her way she would get them seen immediately but that wasn't how things worked. They were understaffed, overworked and — some would argue — underpaid.

On any given day they saw two hundred people flood into the department and even more in the summer months. They tried to keep track of patient flow every four hours and kept turning over the staff every eight but it didn't always work out.

It didn't help that at times it looked as if the nurses weren't doing anything but that wasn't the truth, more often than not it was because rooms were full, they were reviewing blood work, completing charts or looking ahead to see if any preliminary work would make it easier for the doctors.

Jenna recalled one lady a few hours earlier complain that a nurse was eating food at their desk. What she didn't understand was that the nurse hadn't had her break during her shift. Perspective was everything.

She turned to get back to work.

Dr. David Summers emerged through a set of double doors with that permanent frown on his face. They all had them. Fine lines etched into their skin from the constant stress and concern. Even when she went home she found it hard to switch off. It was only after she took the job as a nurse could she begin to understand what Brody was going through when he came home from work and appeared to be ignoring her. It wasn't that. At least that's what he said in counseling. At forty-four, Jenna was sure she'd aged five years since working there, as she'd noticed a few gray hairs streaking through her auburn hair that weren't there before she started the job. However, it was to be expected. Those at the college had warned her of the stress of the job but after working for a zoo, she thought she could handle it.

Dr. Summers glanced at his clipboard, flipping over paper and then surveying the room.

"Anything I can help you with?" Jenna asked.

He exhaled hard and placed the clipboard down, then went over to a computer and brought up an X-ray, followed by some reports on blood work. She was used to being ignored. It wasn't personal. There was only so much room in everyone's mind when they were working. Summers was usually good though and would store away a question and return minutes later with the answer.

"I can't make head or tails of this. That is the sixth patient from Marfa that we have seen today with self-inflicted injuries. One guy stuck a knife into his leg. I asked him why, and he said he just wanted to see what it felt like."

"Crazy," Jenna replied.

He nodded while glancing at the screen with his back to her. "Then there was the lady who walked out in the middle of traffic. She's on life support right now. I'm not sure she'll make it." He turned his head towards her then looked off down the hall.

Jenna thought back to Deidra.

"There has also been a massive upswing of patients today."

"Flu?"

"No, like I said, weird stuff. A few outbursts. Though I have noticed some of the symptoms in those who had hurt themselves were headaches, fever and vomiting. But some had no symptoms, which makes it even stranger. We're running a battery of tests but so far we've got nothing."

Right then they heard a commotion down the hall. It was loud enough that it caught everyone's attention. Heads turned and several patients stepped out into the hallway to see what was going on. It didn't take long for Mary, another nurse, to emerge through a set of doors.

"Where is security when you need them?" she asked.

"What's going on?"

She thumbed over her shoulder. "There is a guy out front who is destroying the seats, and lashing out at people."

Jenna ducked out from behind the counter and made her way down, pushing through the set of double doors into another corridor that took her down to the waiting room. "Shouldn't there be security at the front desk at all times?"

"Yeah, and there should be more doctors," Jenna said.

As they came around a corner that opened up into an expansive space full of seats, a thin guy who looked as if he hadn't slept in days was waving a chair in the air and telling people to get back. "Don't come near me!"

She imagined he would be the one pushing forward but he looked terrified. His eyes were wide, and he was sweating profusely. Was he on drugs? It looked like it. Jenna tried to calm him by putting out a hand and telling him that no one was going to hurt him and if he would just... He tossed the chair at a large man who was edging towards him and in lightning fashion leaped over a line of seats, scooped up another chair and cracked it over the head of another guy who tried to stop him. A black guy fell on the ground, his head now bleeding badly.

"Security!" Jenna yelled.

Realizing the two security guys were gone from their post, she knew she had to try and take control of the situation. From what she could tell he was only attacking people who tried to come near him. He'd walked by two women and though he looked at them he didn't touch them or say anything.

"Listen, no one is going to harm you."

He wasn't listening, he was too focused on another guy who was now furious because he'd injured his friend.

"Get back. Get back!"

Jenna turned to Mary and told her to get a sedative. The only way this guy was going to stop was if he was sedated. The challenge would be getting close enough to administer the injection.

While Mary was away, Jenna tried to get the mans attention but his fight-or-flight instinct kicked in when someone lunged at him. Reacting fast, the crazed man grabbed the guy and swung him into some chairs. Another person tried to overpower him but was injured badly when the 140-pound lunatic threw him into a wall.

Right then Mary returned and handed her the sedative. It wouldn't put him out but it would at least bring down his anxiety a few notches. Jenna had to time it just right. She glanced towards the security booth, wondering where they were. She'd rather they handle it but by the looks of it, if someone didn't act fast, this guy was going to kill someone.

"Jenna. Be careful," Mary said, touching her arm.

She had to admit she'd never felt so scared in her life. When she and Brody were together there were nights she didn't know if he was coming home and that bothered her, but this was on a whole other level. She darted forward just as the man's back was turned and jammed the needle into his backside. He let out a bloodcurdling yell and released his grip on the man and lashed out, but she was already several feet away. She expected him to go nuts.

That momentary distraction was all it took. Another guy managed to slam him into a wall. The sheer force should have knocked him out but he got up and fought back like a wild alley cat, limbs flailing and screeching like a banshee. More chairs were thrown, several hitting women, even a child. Then he turned his attention back to Jenna. His eyes were wild. He charged forward and before she could get a few feet away he took her down and began pummeling a meaty fist into her ribs. She gasped in agony, as each strike was harder than the last. This was followed by one to the face. Fortunately security came barreling into the room and brought him down. The unstable man squirmed beneath them, screaming out that they were going to kill him.

"Sir, stay still. Stop resisting."

In the next second he went as stiff as a board.

It was crazy to watch it play out and had that been it, she might have forgotten about it in a few days, except it was what happened next that concerned her. They dragged him to his feet and began checking his pockets for weapons. While they were doing this, a military truck pulled up outside and several soldiers jumped out of the back, wearing masks and carrying M4s.

"What the heck?" she said, brushing dirt off as they entered through the main doors and began to take charge. They interrupted security and pulled the lunatic away leading him down the hallway. More soldiers, this time in hazmat suits with goggles and respirators, filed into the hospital.

"What are you doing?" Jenna asked pressing forward.

"Stand back, ma'am," a soldier said putting a hand up and making it clear that she was a threat.

"Private, it's okay," said a woman walking in behind several of the soldiers. She carried herself with an air of authority even though she was short in stature. She had bright red hair, and a military uniform on.

Baffled by the intrusion, Jenna persisted. "Would you mind telling me what is going on here?"

"Of course. This place is being quarantined."

Chapter 3

After the couple had shown them where they believed the truck's lights were on the night Viola went missing, the other officer took them back to Alpine leaving Brody and Gottman to venture in Brody's truck across the Mitchell Flat. The couple had seen the lights somewhere between Paisano Pass and the Chinati Mountains. It was a desolate area that spread for miles. The only things out there was desert, the old Marfa Air Field and mountains.

"Dear God, I thought this truck was meant to be top of the line," Gottman said tugging at his collar.

"It goes in tomorrow to get fixed."

"You didn't buy this from the used dealership, did you?"

He glanced at Gottman. There was only one that he was referring to and yes, he bought it there but he wasn't going to tell him that. While he and Gottman were generally on good terms, Gottman had always been a little pissed that he got overshadowed for the position of chief. It was only after that Brody found out that he'd gone for it.

Brody didn't bother to answer him. Instead he flipped the sun visor down and put on his aviators to block the glare of the sun. It was still early but the sun was already drying everything in sight.

"So how you liking the position?" Gottman asked.

"It's not bad."

"Pays well, right? You earning around one ten?"

"About that."

"Nice," he said removing his hat and wiping his brow. Brody knew he was going to bring it up, he'd expected it from the moment he saw him step out of his cruiser. "So I saw your Jenna the other day."

Brody shot him a glance. He didn't like his tone.

"Oh, I mean I had to go to the medical center to deal with some asshole who'd beaten up his wife. I didn't know she was working there. Anyway, we got chatting and uh…she said you and her were divorced."

Brody was quick to reply to that. "Separated. We haven't finalized."

Gottman raised both eyebrows. "Oh man, that's too bad." He didn't sound too bummed out. If Brody wasn't mistaken, it almost sounded fake. "How many years has it been?"

"Twenty-four," Brody replied.

"Wow. That's why I never got married. You see, here's the problem with marriage, Brody. The moment people get that paper in hand, and a ring on that finger, they go batshit crazy." Brody glanced at him and raised a brow so Gottman clarified. "Okay, not immediately but it doesn't take long. You see, people think they have a right to the other person. Before they spewed their vows they wouldn't do half the shit they do once the knot is tied. Then one day you wake up and find out they no longer want to have sex with you, they expect you to pay for their lavish needs, and have you jump whenever they say. Nope. Not me. I'm not into that crap. I date women and that's it. When it gets too serious I dump their ass."

"Even when they're decent?"

"Especially when they are. More often than not it's the quiet ones you have to worry about. They won't say a damn word while you're dating but as soon as you close that door you will see another side to them. Really, it's not the life for any man. We weren't born to be tied down to one woman for our whole lives. Seriously, can you imagine having one flavor of ice cream?" He chuckled to himself and sighed. "Whoever invented marriage was a complete idiot."

"So tell me, Casanova, how do you figure out which one you want to be with then?"

"I don't. Like I said, I date and that's it."

The truck rumbled across the desert, kicking up a plume of dust behind it. It would take them a while to get out to the spot, and well, it was interesting to catch up and see a different view on life. Brody had grown up in a stable family where people stayed together even if they were unhappy. He thought about how unhappy his father was and yet he weathered the storms of his abusive mother.

"Come on, man, you must have met at least one woman you wanted to settle down with?"

Brody bounced in his seat a little as they went over some rough terrain. He swerved the truck around some large boulders.

"Okay, I will admit. There have been a couple but unfortunately they didn't pass the shit test."

Brody laughed. "Run that by me."

"It's a way to filter out those who aren't really interested in you or they are going to be trouble later."

"Like?" Brody probed.

"Like you take a woman out on a date and open the door for them on their side, if they don't lean across and do the same for you, chances are they are going to be a pain in the ass."

"Come on, man, maybe she overlooked it. Are you telling me you have dumped a good woman because she didn't lean across and open your door?"

"Oh yeah. Why should we be the only ones to open

doors?"

"Geesh, Gottman, you must be a real blast on a date."

"What, because I have standards? Believe me, Brody, so do they and they won't think twice about whining about them a year or two into marriage. It's better to nip it in the bud early and avoid all that drama."

"And how do you do that?"

"Okay, let's say you want to give one the benefit of the doubt. Here's three ways you can figure out if they are going to be a pain in the ass later. First test is to see if they would be willing to buy a coffee for you."

"A coffee?"

"Yeah, you've been out on a few dates. Comfort is setting in and you want to know if you can go to that next level. So you take them out and leave your wallet behind and then go through a drive-through and tell them you forgot your wallet, and could they spot you the money. If they willingly do it, you might have a keeper. If she doesn't, perhaps she's too into herself."

"Are you serious?" Brody asked before laughing.

"Please tell me you did not try that on someone."

"Chief, it works. Try it sometime. All right, next one. This is called the No test. Let's say they want to go watch some chick flick, or take you to a museum, and you have zero interest in doing it. Just say no, I'm not interested. If they try to shame you, by saying if you were a real man you would go, drop her ass like a hot rock."

"Hold on a minute, Gottman. You're dealing with another human being here. Are you telling me that you would expect her to go to whatever you wanted but you wouldn't do the same for her? Seems like a double standard there. That has divorce written all over it."

"Is that what happened with Jenna?" he asked before snorting.

Brody shook his head. That wasn't it. Well it kind of was — that and a number of things. Since losing their son Will, so much had changed between them. Her stress, anxiety and all manner of unspoken troubles had worn away at the fabric of their relationship. It wasn't long before they were sleeping in different rooms, and he found Jenna avoiding him. Any time he tried to communicate with her she would just shut him down and tell him that she didn't want to talk about it. Except she would talk about what she wanted. Yep, double standards existed. And it had left both of them broken and empty. He hadn't thought he could feel so much pain and he never expected it to happen to him. Prior to Will's death, they had been on great terms, taking vacations and spending time with one another, and then the loss of their eldest son just tore a giant hole through their entire family. While Brody had managed to heal from it, Jenna hadn't. This led to all manner of arguments and accusations. *Why do you act as though it doesn't affect you? You're so fake; I know you are hurting too!* She couldn't be further from the truth. The fact was it had taken everything inside him to drag himself back to work, and where she saw work as avoiding the problem, to him it was salvation. Something about switching off his personal life and switching on to the work enabled him to cope. If he had to take a wild guess, he was certain that Jenna resented him for that. She wanted him to suffer the way she did. She wanted to see him in tears every night. She wanted him to not want to touch her because how could he enjoy life without Will? But he was a man for God's sake. He had needs. Was he meant to ignore them? The fact was they were still alive. They still had another son that they needed to be strong for. She couldn't see that. So it took her far longer to climb out of the dark hole and scramble back to the land of the living. But by that point they were too damaged. Too many painful words spoken, too many accusations, too many assumptions and too much time apart finally destroyed what had once been a healthy marriage.

It was her that initiated the divorce, not him.

It was her that pulled away.

It was her that moved out.

And it killed him to think that he had lost his closest friend. The person he cared the most about in this damn world.

Brody glanced over at Gottman who was still rattling

away. He forced down his emotions. It didn't take much to get back there. If he broke, it usually happened late at night when he came home to an empty house. Nick had gone to Alpine to live with his mother. Now that relationship was another thing entirely. It came with its own set of challenges. His son had blamed them both. If it wasn't hard enough to lose his brother, he had to witness the breakdown of their marriage.

Gottman continued. "Anyway, the third test you want to try is the prenup. Especially being as a number of us guys are loaded with money and well, you know how women love that credit card."

"Geesh, Gottman, your Tinder profile must be a real hoot."

"Hey, look, it's a short life, do you think women want to spend it with a douche? Well it's a two-way street. I want to enjoy this life, not be dragged down by someone with massive issues."

"Gottman, trust me. You've got issues."

Gottman waved him off and laughed. "Anyway, are we

getting close?"

"Yeah, it's just over this rise."

Right then Officer Matt Niles came over the radio. "Chief. You there?"

Brody scooped up the mic. "Go ahead."

"We seem to be getting a high increase of folks inflicting harm on themselves, and several that are a little out of control, like they're scared."

"And you're calling me because?"

"Well, how do you want us to handle it?"

"Like you would handle any other situation. Your job is to protect and preserve the peace."

"I know, it's just that with Kristin ill at the moment, we're short on staff to hold down the fort. How long are you going to be out there, and any luck finding her?"

"We're still looking." Brody tapped Gottman and muttered to him. "Keep your eyes peeled for anything that looks out of place." He got back on the mic and told Officer Niles to keep him in the loop of how things were progressing, and he encouraged him to use his initiative.

"Proactive policing, Niles, remember that."

"Roger that."

As they came over a rise and swung down into a valley, Brody parked the truck and got out leaving the engine idling. He reached in and pulled out his binoculars and began to scan his field of vision looking for any sign that someone might have been out there digging or might have dumped a body. Chances were if she was dead and someone brought her out there, she was hidden below the earth, or had been tossed down an old mine shaft. The thought of seeing Viola's face made Brody's stomach churn. It wasn't that he couldn't handle seeing death as he'd witnessed it enough over the course of his career, but it never got any easier.

Gottman came around from the passenger side and squinted.

"You see anything?"

"Just a whole lot of desert, rocks and shrubs."

"You know, chief, there is a good chance they didn't even see anyone out here. You know how people are when they see the Marfa lights. Lots of people have their views on what it is."

Brody nodded and they worked their way across the terrain scanning for anything that looked out of place, or where the earth had been disturbed. It took them close to an hour before they stumbled across a patch of land where shrubs had been partially buried as if someone had moved them from one area and replanted them.

"Gottman!" Brody yelled. Gottman was several feet away looking through some old camping gear that someone had left out. It was torn to shreds and weathered by the climate, which made it clear it had been out there a lot longer than a week. "Think I have something."

As Gottman jogged over, Brody began kicking at the earth. The shrubs were loose in the earth. As he continued working the soil and sand, he spotted three fingers sticking out. His heart sank.

Brody crouched and took a moment to catch his breath.

He pulled out a pair of blue latex gloves, took out his

camera and began taking a few snapshots as evidence. He raised a hand towards Gottman to keep his distance, as he wanted to take some video.

Once that was done, over the course of the next five minutes they unearthed the body buried in a shallow grave. Although the earth had begun to decompose the body, Viola looked as if she'd been strangled, as there was purple bruising around her neck.

A warm breeze blew tumbleweed across the ground near their feet and Brody had to put a hand to his face as grit went in his eye. He kept shaking his head as he looked at her soulless eyes. She was still fully clothed but they wouldn't know if a sexual assault had taken place until they got back the initial report from the ME.

"Poor girl, no one deserves to go through this," Gottman said as he rose up and stretched out his back. Brody stooped and took a few more shots of her neck.

"How did you get on with the boyfriend?" Brody asked.

"He's sticking to his story. Seems he has an airtight

alibi. However, we are checking footage from cameras in the area to see if it lines up with his account."

Both of them stared down at the girl. Such a waste of a life, Brody thought. If it happened because there was a breakdown in her relationship, there were always other options. Why people had to go to this extent was beyond him. Sure, his relationship with Jenna hadn't been ideal but at least they both knew when to give each other space. He surveyed the landscape for tire marks.

"I'll look around, there has to be tire tread."

"No, the desert may have taken care of that by now," Brody said.

It was true, all it took was one blustery day and shallow tracks in the ground could be covered up as though a truck had never been there. Five days had already passed. Still, they would need to bring a team out to comb the terrain for tracks. In the meantime he would get in contact with dispatch and get EMTs out here to bag her body.

Chapter 4

Emerick Jones couldn't believe his ears as the last radio caller disconnected. He removed the large black headphones he was wearing, pushed the bulbous sponge microphone away from his face and got up and looked at Angela, his assistant and radio program controller.

"Is the whole world going mad? That's the eleventh phone call we have had this morning telling us about people hurting themselves or lashing out at others."

"Maybe it's all this sun. We have had a bit of a heat wave. My cousin suffered from heat stroke last year. He said he was seeing all manner of things."

"Your cousin is a drunk," Emerick replied walking over to the coffee machine and pouring a cup. "This is very different. I mean, one or two incidents I can accept. In today's society we are dealing with a lot of unstable people, but eleven within a matter of hours?" He crossed the room to the large window that overlooked Highland

Avenue. He took a large gulp of his drink and grimaced. "Shit, Angela, when was the last time you changed this coffee?"

"That was a fresh brew this morning."

He rolled his eyes. "Uh, how many times do I have to remind you? I like my coffee fresh. That's why I get them to do pour overs when I go through Starbucks. None of this pour me a coffee that's been sitting inside a machine for three hours. That crap goes bitter. It gives you a burnt taste."

"Picky."

"If I'm paying four dollars a cup, you had better believe I'm going to be picky. How the hell they get away with it is a mystery."

"Don't go then."

"Easier said than done. I'm addicted to it."

She mumbled something, probably a curse word, and went back to working on lining up what they had next on the agenda. Emerick had been working in radio since he left college. That was forty years ago. A lot had changed since then. Radio was going the way of the dinosaur. Sure they streamed it online and even videoed their guests and uploaded to YouTube but syndicated radio was becoming hard to make a living from. There was so much free stuff out there being created by amateurs that the idea of paying or supporting a radio station was unheard of nowadays. Every week they had to put out a request to have people send in money, he was starting to feel like a local minister asking for tithe. He glanced at his watch; it was a little after two in the afternoon. He was still trying to make heads or tails of what was going on in Alpine and Marfa. Reports had come in from locals who had not only witnessed people losing their mind but others had mentioned seeing a military presence in Alpine.

"Angela, can you get hold of the local hospital in Alpine? Find out what's going on there and see if there is any truth to the rumors."

"I'm on it."

Right then he squinted and stepped closer to the window. "Hey, uh, Angela."

"Yeah?"

"Isn't that David McCarthy?"

Angela turned in her seat and gazed out. "Yeah, what's he doing?"

Emerick chuckled. "Looks like he's had a few too many to drink."

Bar Saint George was on the same block as Marfa Public Radio Station. David was a mechanic in town, a good one at that. Emerick had gone to him on a number of occasions instead of heading into Alpine. He'd worked on his Chevy Blazer a few times and not charged him. Now he was standing out in the middle of the road not moving. Several drivers honked their horns but he didn't react. Then, he began to walk forward towards the oncoming traffic. Vehicles swerved around him, and several drivers shook angry fists at him.

"Here, hold this, I'm going out to speak to him."

Emerick handed off his coffee and walked down the hallway and out a set of doors. The street wasn't that busy, compared to the weekends when everyone and his uncle flooded into town to take in the art galleries and eat at some of the fine restaurants.

"Hey David!" Emerick shouted from the sidewalk.

David turned his head and looked at him and he had this strange look on his face. Almost as if he wasn't registering what was happening. David turned back and continued walking forward. Emerick stepped off the curb to make his way over but a truck shot by nearly striking him. He stumbled back to the sidewalk to catch his breath. Several more vehicles zipped by, preventing him from cutting across. Right then, he heard the roar of an engine, music blaring and then tires squealing and a loud thud. Emerick darted around a large truck that was blocking his view. He hurried out onto the road, and then his stomach sank. Curled up in a fetal position with blood trickling out the side of his mouth was McCarthy.

Standing nearby with hands on his head, a guy was beside himself.

"I didn't see him. I'm sorry. I really didn't see him. I looked down at my phone for just a second and..." The young guy in his mid-twenties trailed off, his face going a ghostly white.

Emerick reached into his pocket and immediately called an ambulance.

"Presidio County Sheriff's Office."

"Hi, I need an ambulance quickly. Send it to South Highland Avenue."

"What's the nature of the emergency?"

"Someone has been struck by a vehicle. Hurry up."

"Sir, we will get one there as soon as we can. However, we are currently experiencing a lag."

"What?" He couldn't believe his ears.

"There is only one ambulance for Marfa and we've had numerous calls over the past few hours. But trust me, they are on their way."

He shook his head and hung up. By now a crowd had gathered, most were staring, someone was trying to perform CPR but without much luck.

"Is an ambulance on the way?" asked Jill Grayson, the owner of Marfa Book Company, a small bookstore just down from the radio station.

Emerick's mind was in a fog. Shock was setting in. "They've been notified but chances of them getting here before…"

The stranger performing CPR stopped and raised his head slowly. "He's gone. There is no pulse."

"Well don't stop. Keep going," Emerick said.

"He's dead."

Emerick dropped to his knees and shoved the man out of the way and began applying pressure to David's chest. With each chest compression, more blood came gushing out of David. He got close and listened but there was nothing. No breathing. He was gone. Emerick leaned back on his knees and looked into the bright blue Texas sky. Someone placed a hand on his shoulder and he turned to find Angela beside him. "Emerick. There's nothing more you can do."

A few people stepped in to lift David's body out of the road onto the sidewalk while Emerick walked back across to the station. He was shaken up by the ordeal and needed a drink. Something stiff. Something to take the edge off.

He kept shaking his head. "I just don't get it. Why would he just walk out in front of traffic? It doesn't make sense."

* * *

Across town, Nick was in his second to last class of the day. There had been rumors spreading among the students that the military was in town conducting some kind of training for some doomsday event. Keith Parker, a kid who often arrived late because he lived in Alpine but traveled to Marfa for school, said his old man was nearly stopped on the way out of Alpine. They had seen police and several military officials stopping vehicles but his dad had managed to find an alternative route out.

Then to add even more fuel to the rumors, sick videos of locals injuring themselves were circulating online. One showed a guy sticking a knife through his hand, another was of someone dousing himself with gasoline and setting himself on fire, and then another was of someone trying to attack people with a machete. That video was cut short when police started shooting.

Of course it was speculation. Everyone knew that videos online were often doctored to look real. Now had that been all that had happened, he might not have given it another thought, but they'd already had a kid in gym class that morning hit the button to retract the telescopic bleachers and then he shoved his hand inside as it was closing. Apparently it was a mess. Nick had already hit the showers by then but he heard the scream, and by the time he went to see, the teachers had already closed off the room but Shelly Winthrop saw it and passed out. They carted her away, and an ambulance took her to the hospital to treat her for trauma.

"Hey, Jackson," Devan said under his breath as he shot him a glance and kept low so the teacher couldn't see he was talking. They were meant to be studying and working on algebra but Nick couldn't shake the weird feeling that something big was happening.

"What?"

"You want to nip down to the gym and see if we can get in there?"

"Don't be stupid. They have it blocked off."

"I think the kid killed himself."

"That's not what I heard. Jerry said they took him away in an ambulance."

"Yeah, in a body bag," he said with a grin on his face.

"Jones!" a loud voice bellowed. "Do I have to put you outside?"

Devan looked around and made a waving gesture to Mr. Harper before pretending to look interested in his work again. Mr. Harper's eyes darted to Nick and he returned to scanning his study book.

"Psst," Devan said.

"What?"

"So?"

"Seriously, man, just focus," Nick said glancing at Harper who fortunately had his head down.

"Nah, meet me outside in five. Tell him you need the washroom."

Devan's chair let out a screech as he got up and went to the front of the room to be excused. Harper glanced over his glasses and shook his head but then flicked his hand towards the door. Devan smiled. At the door he mimicked himself being hanged before darting out. Nick shook his head and was about to return to studying when he caught Callie looking at him. He coughed and cleared his throat. She always had this way about her that made his throat go dry. Nick glanced at the clock on the wall. There wasn't long until the end of the day. His father had arranged to take him to the movies that night. It frustrated him to no end the way things had gone between his parents. They both used him like pawns in a game. One of them would do something nice, and the next would up the ante once they learned about it as if they were scared he would pick sides. He didn't want to be in the middle of it all but he had no choice. He just wished they could work it out.

Nick sat there for a few more minutes until he saw Devan's head appear at the door. He ducked the second

Harper turned, and then reappeared a few seconds later gesturing for him to come.

"Mr. Jackson. Do we have a problem?"

"Uh. No, sir. Actually I was hoping I could use the washroom."

"You as well? In my time, we had to hold it until the end of class."

"I really need to go," he said as he winced and gave his best impression of needing a piss.

"Fine. Just make it quick and find out where Jones has gone. Damn boy spends more time in the washroom than in my lectures."

"Will do," Nick said rising and glancing at Callie, who brushed her hair behind her ear and smiled. He felt his heart pound a little harder before he ducked out. As soon as he was outside and halfway down the hall, he felt a hand grab him and yank him back.

"Shhh! Or I'll slit your throat," Devan said before cracking up laughing.

"Seriously, you have mental problems."

"Don't we all. C'mon!" He jogged down the empty corridor full of steel lockers on either side. The walls were coated in a thick off-white color, and had a green band that went horizontal. It didn't take them long to get over to where the gym was. The door had a huge thick lock on it.

"Great. See. Told you. Now let's get back," Nick said.

"Oh ye of little faith." With that said, Devan pulled out of his pocket a small plastic container and flipped it open to reveal a lock picking set.

"Seriously? That stuff doesn't work."

"It doesn't if you're an idiot," he replied crouching down and jamming two small steel rods into the lock. "Keep an eye out. This might take a little bit of time." He began working on it while Nick peered down the hallway. He knew Harper wouldn't let them be out there long before he'd hunt them down. Then next thing heard was the sound of the lock coming off.

"Voilà!" Devan said all proud of himself. He yanked the thick chain off and pushed through into the gymnasium. Nick ducked inside and his eyes fell on the now open bleachers.

"Devan, this is nuts."

"I'm telling you something is going on. People are freaking out and acting strange. I mean, who the hell jams their hand inside closing bleachers, or jumps inside a lions' den?"

"Those with mental health issues."

"Yeah but then how do you explain all those accounts of people in Alpine and Marfa recently?"

They jogged over and Devan scanned the area like he was on an Easter egg hunt. He had a look of glee on his face as if expecting to see something real gnarly.

"I told you. They would have cleaned it up."

Devan jumped up onto the bleachers and Nick watched as he ran up a few and then ducked down and slipped between them. "What are you doing?"

He saw his cell phone light switch on, and then within seconds, he said, "Bingo! Nick. Come see this."

"I don't think I want to."

"Nick."

Nick groaned and hurried up the steps and slipped between them. As he dropped down he caught sight of what Devan was illuminating with his light. It was blood that was still on the bleachers themselves. They'd cleaned it off the floors but missed a spot.

"See, I told you."

Right then they heard the doors open in the gymnasium.

"Devan Jones. Nick Jackson. Out now!"

They stood there frozen, unsure if they should pretend to not be there and hope that Harper went away, but once they heard his footsteps making his way over they knew the gig was up.

"I said out!"

Nick knew this would happen. They crawled out and brushed themselves off as they made their way down to the waxed floor. "This is detention for both of you, and Jones…" Harper put his hand out and at first Devan tried to act like he had nothing but then he pulled out the lock pick set and handed it over.

"Right, head on out."

Outside in the hall Harper berated them and told them this was going to leave a big mark on their record. He was laying the fear on heavy. He was known for doing that. It was all bull crap but he thought it worked. The guy was old school and if he had his way he would have advocated for corporal punishment but it had been taken out of the school system, thank God. Well, at least in quite a few states. When they reentered the classroom and were told to take a seat, he noticed that Toby Winters wasn't there. "Anyone know where Winters is?"

"He just walked out a few minutes after you," Callie said.

"Okay, well stay here. I will be right back." He sighed. "They don't pay me enough to do this crap." Once he was out of the room Devan rolled into his speech about how he'd found the severed hand of the kid beneath the bleachers.

"Bullshit," someone said.

Devan pulled out his phone and showed them the snapshot he'd taken. Right then several of the students in the room hurried over to the window and looked out. "Hey, check this out. That's Winters." A few kids started laughing as Nick went over and looked. Sure enough there was Toby Winters. He'd climbed up onto the roof of the building and was walking along the edge. Down on the ground, Harper and the caretaker were trying to get him to come down.

"Hell yeah!" Devan said pumping his fist in the air. "Rage against the man."

"No, something's not right," Callie said. "He was acting all out of sorts. You know, looking into space earlier on as if he was in some kind of trance state. I snapped my fingers near him and he jumped back looking petrified as if I was going to kill him."

"Ah, so this is all your fault, Callie," Devan said before laughing.

Everyone in that moment just thought this was a kid acting out, trying to make a point, but Nick knew otherwise. Toby Winters wasn't the class clown. He was a straight A student. When it came to studies and school he was all business. Unlike Devan who took every chance he could get to slack off.

Someone in the class opened a window so they could hear what was going on. Nick got closer and watched as several teachers came out and tried to coax Toby into coming down but he wasn't listening. He looked like a tightrope walker balancing on the lip of the school building making his way to the far end. Students began making assumptions.

"You think he's going to jump?"

"The kid must have home issues."

"It's all the pressure. Probably his old man reamed him out after he got a B instead of an A." Chatter spread across the knot of students as they pressed forward. All of a sudden, everyone stopped breathing as Toby stepped off the edge and hurtled to the ground. Nick winced at the sight.

His impact on the concrete was palpable.

Chapter 5

What was the military doing here? Emerick had been sitting in the radio station for the past ten minutes expecting an ambulance to appear. He was staring out the window, his hand shaking as he sipped on a glass of bourbon, when the large green military truck rolled up the street and multiple soldiers hopped out the back, rifles at the ready, directing the people to step away from McCarthy's body. The look of fear and confusion on bystanders' faces was evident as they took control of the situation. The soldiers weren't geared up in regular attire; they had respirator masks, goggles and gloves as if they were treating some kind of pathogen.

"Angela, check this out."

She'd returned to setting up some of their pre-programmed shows so they could take the rest of the day off. She came over and glanced out. "What the hell?"

"When was the last time you called for an ambulance

and they sent the military?"

"Those rumors about Alpine must be true," she said.

They loaded the limp body of McCarthy into the back of the truck and then approached several of the people that had been close to him when they arrived. Emerick couldn't hear the conversations but it was clear that there was some disagreement as the two men and one woman who'd been close began raising their arms, shouting and backing away. Their attempts to leave were met with resistance. A soldier grabbed one of the guys by the arm and the man responded by wheeling around and punching him in the side of the head. All hell broke loose. Rifles were raised, hands went in the air, and within seconds the three were thrown down on the ground and zip tied. Meanwhile curious spectators looked on bewildered by it all. Emerick couldn't believe his eyes as the woman and the two men were strong-armed to the back of the truck and thrown inside. He had a good mind to go out there and protest with the crowd but that idea went out the window once he saw Jill Grayson point at the radio station. One of the soldiers looked their way. Their only saving grace was that the window had a tint to it, otherwise they would have seen them staring back. Two soldiers made their way across the street heading towards the radio station. Like a light turning on, Emerick came to his senses and began backing up. "Angela. We need to get out of here now."

"Why? What's going on?"

"No time to explain. Let's go!"

He grabbed her by the hand and yanked her to the back of the room, he shouldered through a door and they hurried down a corridor and slammed into the emergency exit. As soon as they were out the back he made a beeline for his Chevy Blazer that was parked a few feet away.

"Emerick. We haven't done anything."

"Yes we have. We came in contact with McCarthy. Those three other people were also touching and close to him."

"But I never…"

She looked at him and then realized she'd touched

Emerick. They hopped into the Blazer, fired up the engine and reversed out, tires squealing before he crushed the accelerator pedal and tore out of the back alley. The Chevy bounced off the curb and onto El Paso Street. Businesses were a blur as he powered away, trying to put as much distance as he could between them and the station.

"This is crazy, Emerick. Stop the vehicle."

"You saw what happened back there. You heard the radio broadcasts, and watched those videos online. Something is going down and I don't intend to get caught up in it. I need to get my kid and then reassess the situation."

* * *

Brody and Gottman carried Viola out of that rocky ravine. Under any normal circumstances they would have left her there and got the medical examiner to come out and seal off the area but there was a fear that whoever had done this might return and dispose of the body. It wasn't uncommon for someone to dump a body and return later to transfer it elsewhere. But that wasn't the biggest concern they had. When Brody had contacted dispatch to get an EMT to meet them out at the main highway, they were told that EMTs weren't going out as the dispatcher had been having a hard time connecting with them. It made no sense. Even at their busiest time in Alpine there was always someone who would at least take the call. Brody told the dispatcher they would take her body to the ME's office and to not worry.

They were within half a mile from the vehicle and had stopped to take a break when Gottman spoke up. He had taken out his phone and was trying to get a signal.

"Chief, you know I'm not even getting one bar out here."

"We're too far out. Wait until we get back to the highway."

"I wanted to get in touch with the department and find out what's going on in Alpine."

"It's probably just a breakdown of communication."

"When has that ever happened?"

"Look, just give me a hand carrying her back."

Gottman wiped sweat from his brow and with a sour look on his face grabbed Viola's legs. They continued on, shuffling across the desert plain. The afternoon heat was making his shirt stick to his back and the constant yapping by Gottman was starting to get on his last nerve. At the back of his mind, Brody knew he was going to have to give a death notification to the family and he hated doing that. The amount of training they gave them at the academy amounted to half a paragraph, that's because there was no easy way to drop it on a family. All you could do was express your sympathy, ask them if there was someone who could stay with them and then reassure them that the department was doing everything they could to resolve it, if it was related to murder. Murders were the toughest cases of them all because there were no guarantees.

Brody had wrapped a handkerchief around his face because the smell of the decaying body was awful. "So hey, I was thinking, with you and Jenna breaking up and all. Would you mind if…?"

Brody's eyebrow went up as Gottman trailed off.

"Are you kidding me?" Brody said.

"No. I know it's fresh right now. I was meaning in time. Six months from now if she's still single."

"I haven't signed the papers."

"But you plan on it."

"Gottman."

"Right. I'm sorry. Just she's a great-looking gal and I would hate to see that all go to waste."

Brody had tried to not think about Jenna. It was easier to shut her out of his mind. In the first few days after she left he couldn't work. He just couldn't get his head into focusing. He wasn't a man given to crying but something broke inside of him after she walked out that day. He wouldn't have minded if she wanted to keep an open line of communication but she shut him down, cut him off and made it seem as if there was no way forward. For the first time in his life he'd felt out of control. Like his world was falling apart and twenty-four years had been flushed down the drain. He would walk through the day like a ghost, doing the bare minimum to survive. He spent hours talking to his family but there was nothing they could do except console him and tell him to give her time. She'll come around. She always does, they would say. But something inside told him different. It wasn't just a disagreement. It was her mental anguish over the death of Will. She had never really got help for it. Whereas him, he'd had the police services psychiatrist to bounce his thoughts off, but Jenna had avoided the idea of speaking to anyone. Perhaps thinking time would heal the wound but it hadn't.

Brody felt the muscles in his arms weaken as they carried Viola the last leg of the journey. His truck was now in sight, which was a relief. He glanced at Gottman and shook his head. The nerve of the guy. Only two months after she had walked out and he was already looking to scoop her up. It pissed him off but on the other hand, he didn't blame him. Jenna was a good-looking woman. It was the reason why she'd caught his attention back when they were in their late teens. She was stunning. Something about that long hair, her green eyes and reserved character was massively attractive. And yet even though time had put wrinkles on both of their faces, he could still see that young girl buried beneath the years. He missed her. He missed the woman he'd married. That's why he couldn't bring himself to sign the papers. His mind kept churning over every good memory in his head. Every vacation, every glance and every moment they laughed together. How could he give that up? He'd forever be searching for her in other women, if he could even bring himself to love anyone else again.

"Well I have never been more glad to see your truck," Gottman said as they laid Viola on the ground and Brody opened the rear and they carefully placed her into the back. He covered her with a blue tarp and shut the door. The wind blew grit in his eyes, and tumbleweed rolled across the terrain. He gazed up into the blue sky, where only a few clouds drifted slowly across the horizon.

"So who do you think is behind it?"

"No idea," Brody replied.

"C'mon, you must have a gut instinct."

He stared back at him.

"Without solid evidence, my instincts are just that, instincts that I keep to myself. And you would be wise to do the same thing," Brody said as he came around to the driver's side and hopped in. He fired up the motor and once Gottman was in, they peeled out leaving behind a plume of dust. It didn't take them long to get back to US-90. Brody exited the desert plain and headed northeast on the thirty-minute drive into Alpine.

"Where is everyone?" Gottman said, noticing there was no one on the road. Sure, Marfa was in the middle of nowhere and there was a good twenty miles between towns but they usually passed by at least one vehicle. In the ten minutes they'd been driving they hadn't seen anyone, not even an RV on the roadside. Something seemed off about it all, especially in light of dispatch saying what they had. Brody pulled off to the side of the road as he saw military trucks in the distance. Although he could have driven into town and logic would tell him that it was probably nothing, the military didn't show up in their neck of the woods without good reason.

* * *

Back at the school, everyone was still in shock after witnessing Winters' suicide. But it was what happened next that caused everyone to chatter. Multiple military trucks rolled into the school grounds, fanning out in every direction. Soldiers bounced out, rushing forward. All of them were outfitted in hazmat suits, bearing rifles and preparing for a confrontation. If that wasn't bad enough, several phones throughout the class started ringing, one of which was Devan's.

"It's my old man. Hold tight," he said turning away and answering it.

Nick listened in on several conversations people were having. From what he could grasp it was their parents.

"Yes, I'm here at the school," someone replied.

"I'm not going anywhere."

"Mom, you are worrying me. Calm down."

"Dad, where? You want me to meet you?" Devan asked.

Nick stared out trying to make sense of the odd sight of soldiers patrolling through the school grounds. They approached Mr. Harper and got into a conversation before he was led away and placed in the back of the truck. In fact, all of them were. At least those who were close to Winters.

Right then, Nick felt a firm hand on his shoulder. It was Devan.

"My old man says he's on his way to pick me up. He says the military are in town as well." His mouth remained agape as he looked out seeing soldiers approaching the school. "He says it's not safe and we need to get out. I'm meeting him over at Coffield Park. You coming?"

Nick frowned. "Um, I...I need to get in touch with my mother."

Devan thumbed over his shoulder. "You can do that later. We need to get out of here."

"Hold on a second. There is probably a rational reason for this," Callie chimed in.

"Yeah, and there was probably a rational reason why Winters just swan dived off the roof too but that didn't end well, and I'm not sticking around to see what those soldiers want," Devan said turning and grabbing up his bag and making a beeline for the door. "You coming or not, Jackson?"

Nick looked at Callie, shrugged, grabbed up his bag and made a run for it.

As soon as they were in the hallway, they could hear yelling, and what sounded like a gun going off. Nick's eyes widened and they bolted heading for the west side of the school. Coffield was close, about ten minutes away from the school by foot. They hurried down one hallway and were just about to cross into another and go through a set of double doors when Nick spotted soldiers coming in from the other side. He grabbed Devan and pulled him back into a washroom just in the nick of time.

Chapter 6

Outside they heard the sound of yelling and soldiers ordering people to stay where they were. This was followed by another gunshot. Devan was freaking out trying to text his father while Nick stood by the door with it partially cracked. He couldn't believe this was happening; it was like something straight out of a movie. He turned and looked towards the window then shook his head. There was no way they were getting out of that, it was too narrow. He entered a stall while Devan continued to rant about how the government had to be behind all this and how his father had told him that one day they would take over. "It's martial law. This is where it begins. The downfall of America."

"Devan, keep it down."

He lifted up one of the ceiling tiles to gauge how much space was above it. The chances of them being able to walk out of the building without being stopped were slim so their only chance was to hide.

"You think you can fit up there?"

"Are you serious? I am not going up there."

Above the ceiling tiles, thick dusty pipes snaked away into darkness. Nick reached up and checked to see if they were hot. They were cold. He hauled himself up by standing on the toilet's tank and using the wall as a support. While he tested it out he continued talking. "I figure we have minutes before they start locking this school down and performing a search."

"Why would they do that?"

"Toby Winters."

"The guy leapt to his death. What the hell do we have to do with that?"

"Don't you see? He leapt to his death, the kid in the gymnasium jammed his hand in the bleachers, there are videos of people doing all manner of weird shit all over the county and then we had that incident the other day at the zoo. Ourselves and everyone else have been in contact with them."

He hauled himself up into the tight spot and wrapped his leg over a pipe and then tried to put the ceiling tile into place. It was possible. It was tight but it could work at least for now.

"Devan. Get up here now."

Devan went over to the door and cracked it ever so slightly. Within seconds he turned and hurried to get up into the same spot just one over from him. "They are everywhere, going room to room, bringing kids out."

They pulled the ceiling tiles back into place and waited there in the dark, resting on top of the thick pipes in an awkward position. "So you think this is some kind of virus, disease or such?" Devan asked.

"They're wearing masks, goggles, gloves. What do you think?"

"So we're infected?"

"I don't know," Nick said, turning on his cell to provide a smidgen of light. He turned the brightness down low, just enough so they could see one another and he could look online to see what was happening. If the military had taken over the town, there had to be some kind of general alert put out. The first thing he accessed was the local news website. Nothing. No article, no video, no headline on the first page. "All I know is that these kinds of events don't end well, especially for small towns like ours. You heard what the news said. That guy in El Paso was from our town. So it makes sense that they would be coming here. They probably think we're infected with whatever that guy had."

"So it is infectious," Devan said.

"Devan, I haven't a clue right now, I'm just…"

He was just about to finish when they heard a door open and slam against the wall, and a deep gruff voice bellowed, "Check the stalls."

They stared at each other for a second before Nick turned off his phone.

Below they could hear someone kicking each of the doors on the stalls.

Nick swallowed hard, a bead of sweat trickled down his temple.

"No one's here."

"All right. Let's go."

The sound of footsteps against the tiled floor, and then they were gone. The door closed and then Devan's phone started ringing. Nick's eyes widened, and Devan wrestled to get his phone out of his pocket to turn it off. He hit silence just as the door reopened. Both of them froze, as the sound of boots slowly walking back through the washroom got closer. Whoever was down there had stopped walking. Nick held his breath and prayed to God that they didn't start searching the ceiling.

"Private. You're wanted out here."

"I thought I heard something."

"Soldier."

"Yes, sir."

The sound of him leaving was a welcome relief but they couldn't be sure he was gone so they remained there for several minutes not moving until Nick decided to take a look. "They're gone." He put the ceiling tile back into place and Devan texted his father to tell him only to text from now on and that they were trapped right now but would meet him at the park as soon as they could get out.

"Who you calling?" Devan asked, seeing Nick on the phone.

"Trying to get hold of my father. If anyone is going to know what's happening it's him."

He tried but his call just went to voicemail.

Hi, this is Chief Brody Jackson. Sorry I missed your call. Leave your name and number at the beep and I will get back to you shortly.

"Damn it."

* * *

Harry's Tinaja was a bar with a lot of character located on the main drag in Alpine's downtown. It was unique in that it offered loaner guitars that patrons could play at their table, and had by far the cheapest beer in town. It was also a perfect place to chat without anyone eavesdropping. Sergio Leon sat in the far corner, waiting on a friend — his mind churning over the past week and the death of Viola. He twisted the glass of ale in front of him and eyed the patrons with a look of disgust and skepticism. The image of Viola's last moments replayed in his mind like a movie; the sweet loving call to invite her over for dinner, locking the doors on his apartment and bringing up the topic of her extracurricular activities without him. He'd seen the way she'd changed. Hiding her passwords from him. Keeping her phone out of reach. In the fourteen months he'd been dating her he thought they had something going, something strong, he'd even introduced her to his family thinking that one day they'd walk down the aisle together. But that wasn't to be. No, she wanted to move away. Go to a different college. See other people. Of course she wouldn't come out with it. But it was clear. She'd stopped inviting him to nights out and then the lies started. He could feel his blood boiling inside of him at the thought of it. He recalled the night she'd told him she was staying home only to find her with a group of friends, some of which were guys, down at the local movie theater. He hadn't approached her but took the opportunity to ask her the next day how her night in had gone. Sure enough she lied.

This wasn't how it was meant to go.

She wasn't meant to pull away, walk away and lead another life.

He had other plans — plans of them getting a place together, finishing college and settling down in Alpine, but that wasn't to be. Then he finally caught her. Caught her with another man. She said it was just a friend but that was bullshit. She knew how much it riled him up to see her hanging out with other guys.

For that she would pay.

A glass shattered, breaking his train of thought and setting his nerves on edge. He glanced over to see Harry getting out a broom to sweep it up. He apologized and everyone returned to their mundane chatter. *C'mon, Lars, where the hell are you?* he thought as he took a large gulp of his drink and recalled the night she breathed her last breath. He'd managed to convince her to head back to his apartment for a meal. He'd buttered her up telling her that he thought it was good that she was going to study elsewhere and that maybe she was right. Perhaps, it was best they saw other people and gave each other the freedom they wanted. She fell for it hook, line and sinker.

He'd considered not doing the deed, gone back and forth in his mind, but her betrayal was too much. She needed to understand that she couldn't just draw people in then throw them away like they were nothing more than an old rag. He had a heart. He felt. It hurt like hell.

She arrived, and he locked the door behind her and took her coat. She wandered through his apartment one final time soaking it in but turning up her nose as if turned off by what she once found great. She turned and smiled. Oh, he planned to wipe the smile off her face. The dinner was just a ruse to get her comfortable. He'd turned the music on real loud so the neighbors couldn't hear her screams and then he called her out on her lies.

The look on her face was priceless.

She knew what was coming, he was sure of that but it was too late.

Instead of answering him she went to the door to get

her coat, but she never made it. He pounced on her from behind. She fought him as he pinned her to the ground, wrapped his hands around her throat and told her she was a bad person and the world would be a better place without her in it. Seconds turned to minutes before she stopped kicking.

He watched as the light went out in her eyes and the sense of satisfaction kicked in.

All that was left after was to dispose of the body. He'd wrapped her up in bed sheets and called his friend Lars Randall. There were very few people he could rely on but Lars was one of them. Through good and bad, they'd had each other's backs and the death of Viola was no different.

Lars had the truck and Sergio knew a good spot out near the mountains. He'd camped there countless times over the years. It was isolated, barren and far from the regular trails. It was going to be her final resting place, a spot he could revisit from time to time to reminisce, but that was then, before the cops started sniffing around his property. They'd already been over his place with a fine-tooth comb but they wouldn't find anything. Any hair fibers, blood or anything that tied Viola to his place was all circumstantial. She'd been there hundreds of times. Of course her DNA would be there. It was his word against theirs and with his father a lawyer in Alpine with deep connections, he didn't see this going any further than a month.

The door to the bar opened, flooding the inside with daylight as Lars stepped in and looked around. Sergio eyed him and he made his way over, threading around small round tables and a couple of sleazy chicks dancing. Lars slipped in across from him and sighed removing his baseball cap. He was in his early twenties, a mechanic by trade, and so his hands were always covered in grease even long after he'd cleaned them.

"So? I thought you didn't want us to be seen together?"

"I didn't. But things have changed. I need you to give me a hand to get rid of *it*."

He knew what he meant.

"I thought *it* was already gone!"

"The cops pulled me in for questioning twice now. They are honing in on me. It's only a matter of time before they put two and two together and…"

"They don't know squat," Lars said raising his hand to gesture to the waiter to come over and take his order.

"There are only two people who know about this."

Lars squinted at him. "You think I would say something?"

Sergio shrugged. "People do a lot of things when they're under pressure."

"I would be throwing myself under the bus. Why would I do that?"

"To get a better deal."

Lars snorted. "You are paranoid. Look, it wasn't me who did the deed. I didn't have to help you but I did. If you can't trust me we are done."

Sergio studied him trying to see a crack in his veneer. He wouldn't think twice about killing his friend if he knew he was going to give him up to the cops.

"Listen," Sergio said leaning across the table. "Are you going to help or not?"

"Of course I will. We are in this together."

"So we do it tonight."

"Can't be tonight."

"Why?"

"Didn't you see the police presence out on the roads? The military in town?"

"So, even more reason to do it. They will be distracted."

"I think you're missing the point here. Something is going on. They have set up checkpoints on the north, east and west sides of town."

"So we take your truck and head south. We have to go south anyway."

A waitress came over and interrupted him, asking for his order. He asked for a beer and she smiled before walking away. Lars stared at her ass like he always did.

"I don't know, man. It's risky. Besides, I was chatting

to a buddy of mind down at the garage and he said his cousin is being held at the hospital because they have the place on lockdown."

"So they're worried about a virus or something. Look, who gives a shit? We need to dispose of it, immediately. The cops have been sniffing around my place and I'm pretty damn sure they have someone watching me."

"And how do you intend to do that?"

"I have my ways. You'll see."

"In the meantime, you still got that Glock?"

"Why?"

"I'm not going down for this, and if we get caught…"

"You're going to shoot yourself?"

"Hell no. But I sure as hell won't think twice about dropping a cop."

"And if they close in on you?"

"Like said, I'm not doing time. I couldn't handle it inside."

Lars looked at him as the waitress returned with his drink and dropped it off. He thanked her and slapped her on the ass as she walked away. He wouldn't have got away with it had it been anyone else but Lars had dated her at one time and he liked to make it clear that he was still interested.

They clinked their glasses together.

He was free and he wasn't going to let anyone change that, including his pal.

Chapter 7

"Is the coast clear?" Devan asked peering over Nick's shoulder as he checked for the third time. Soldiers were going room-to-room and bringing students down to the main gymnasium. Nick threw up a hand to make it clear they needed to wait. It was all about timing. One mistake and they would find themselves staring down the barrel of a gun. It seemed almost too unreal to believe that this was happening. Not in their school. Not in their town. Nothing big ever happened here. The plan was simple, they would sprint to the next room, a room he'd seen that had already been cleared, and continue to do that until they reached an exit or they found a room where they could exit via one of the windows. Nick was well aware that they might have to change their game plan but they couldn't remain where they were. Devan's father wouldn't wait for them forever.

"Okay, let's go!" Nick said dashing out of the

bathroom, not even waiting to see if Devan was following. His heart was thumping in his chest, his thoughts raced as he put his head down and kept his back against the wall and moved at a fast pace towards the nearest classroom. Even though he knew it had been cleared, he still expected to find a soldier in there. It was strange how the mind worked. It could hang on to hope and entertain disaster all at the same time.

As soon as he was in the door, Devan barreled in after him. They stayed low to the ground and made their way over to a window. Outside they could see even more military trucks than before. It was like they had fanned out, expecting students to run.

"This is not good, not good at all," Devan muttered with a look of fear and apprehension. "How the hell are we supposed to get by them?"

"They can't be surrounding the whole school," Nick replied.

"Well it sure as hell looks like it."

Nick kept looking back over his shoulder, expecting to

be caught. His anxiety was through the roof. Jogging at a crouch they headed back to the door and peered through the glass. "You ready to move?" Nick said.

"No. But what choice do we have? I think I'm going to be sick," he said before curling over and gagging. Nick placed a hand on his back.

"Hang in there, buddy."

He cracked the door open and peered out one last time before grabbing Devan by the collar and dragging him out. They dashed to the next classroom and proceeded to do the same for another four more classrooms until they could see the exit. A wave of relief over having not been caught so far washed over him only to be replaced by disappointment when he saw a large chain and lock on the door.

"Oh you have got to be kidding me!" Nick said.

"What?"

"They've locked the door."

Devan obviously didn't believe him as he had to see it for himself. He exhaled hard. "We are screwed. We might as well just hand ourselves in."

"Hold on a minute, weren't you the one ready to get out of here?"

"That was until seeing they'd locked this place down like Fort Knox."

"They might be able to lock doors but they can't lock windows."

"No, but they have no need to when they have a fleet of military vehicles outside, and armed soldiers patrolling the school." Nick hurried over to the window and looked out. He'd done this in each of the classrooms to get a better idea of how the military was tackling this.

"Look, they aren't going to hold people in the gymnasium for long. They are probably keeping them there while they perform a roll call to ensure that no one has slipped away. After which they'll load them up and cart them out of here. We don't have long before they realize we aren't there but are in the building somewhere." Nick returned to the door to keep watch on what was happening. There was a commotion out in the hallway and in the gap they saw Thomas Barnum making a run for it down the corridor. In the grip of panic and casting a glance over his shoulder to keep an eye on his pursuers, he didn't see a soldier step out ahead of him and raise an arm to clothes hang him. His feet went out from underneath him and he landed hard on his back only a few feet away from their door. He was coughing and spluttering. Two soldiers laid into him with batons before placing a knee on his back and zip tying him. As they were putting him into restraints, Barnum's head was forced at an angle so that his field of vision had them in it. His eyes widened as he saw Nick hiding. He mouthed the word *run* before the soldiers hauled him to his feet and carted him off back to the gymnasium.

A shot of cold fear coursed through Nick.

He'd never seen someone so afraid.

They had to get out of there and now.

"Devan, you remember that room Gypsy allowed us to have a cigarette in?"

"Yeah."

"There was a hatch that went up to the roof area. If we can get up there we'll have a better view of where the military is and potentially determine a way out without getting seen. Right now we can't see shit from down here."

"But the caretaker's room is three corridors away. We don't stand a chance in hell of making it there. We're lucky we even made it this far."

"You have a better idea?" Nick asked.

Devan stared back, biting down on his lower lip and then biting his nails. He shook his head. "Okay, let's do this."

Gypsy was a caretaker who worked at the school for many years until they fired him for letting students smoke in the boiler room. He'd often use it as a place to listen to music, smoke a joint or eat his lunch, and because he got on well with lots of the students, he didn't think twice about letting others join him there. He would often offer students cigarettes and allowed a small group of students, including Nick and Devan, to join him there at lunch break from time to time. That was until another student ratted them out and the principal shut the whole thing down and fired the poor guy. The caretaker now was a complete asshole. Still, Nick remembered what the room looked like. Essentially all the heating and guts of the school was contained inside it. It smelled nasty, like grease and steel, but for a long time it was a great place to have a smoke without teachers knowing. Gypsy would crack open a hatch at the top of a rusted ladder and use a fan to blow out the smoke, while putting a towel at the bottom of the door to avoid teachers smelling anything. Maybe the plan would go south on them but it was worth a shot and right now that was all they could do. Now they just had to get down three corridors. He muttered under his breath, you can do this. As confident as he was in front of Devan, he would be lying to say he didn't have his doubts.

Like mice trying to escape cats they darted in and out of classrooms, moving as fast as they could. Multiple times they nearly got caught, especially on the second hallway. A soldier had walked into view but was looking down at his phone while they were fully exposed with their backs to the walls. Had he turned to his left he would have seen them but fortunately he walked on.

Then there was the last stretch before the boiler room.

Two soldiers had been posted at the far end of the hallway and for a brief moment, Nick thought it was over. Then, as if fate would have it, a commotion further down the hall drew them away leaving a small window of opportunity.

They took it.

Like two Olympic runners in a 100-meter race, they pounded the ground, legs pumping like pistons as they raced forward knowing that if they didn't do it then, there was a good chance the moment would be gone forever.

By the time they slipped into the boiler room both of them were sweating and panting hard. Devan curled over placing his hands on his knees and trying to catch his breath.

"Holy crap, I thought for sure they would look back."

"Look, we don't have much time," Nick said as they made their way over to the ladder and prepared to climb. They were just about to ascend when the door rattled behind them and opened wide.

* * *

"We would like to know what is going on!" Dr. Summers said, rising to his feet before being told to sit down by a soldier. Since the arrival of the military at Alpine Medical Center, much of the staff had been isolated, except for a few who were brought into a separate room and not told why. Jenna was one of them, as was Dr. Summers. The rest were nurses, and higher-up management. They had been given water bottles, had their cell phones removed and had been told they would get answers, but for now they were to remain where they were. As the hours wore on, so their patience became thin.

"I have a daughter at home that is expecting me back," Trish Warren said. She was a nurse whose shift was over two hours ago. The three armed soldiers standing at the front of the room just remained stoic and unmoved by her outburst.

Jenna placed a hand on Trish's arm and tried to get her to relax. "There's no point inciting them. I have to get back for my kid but until they…"

Before she had finished what she was saying, the door opened and in walked two people, the woman she'd seen earlier and a taller gentleman dressed in military attire.

"Thank you for being patient. I understand you have questions and we are here to answer them but please understand that this matter is of national security and so there are some things we can't share with you at this time. My name is Colonel Nichol Lynch and this is Major Tim Brown."

"What the hell is going on?" Summers asked.

"The medical center is being quarantined for a short period of time until we have conducted an investigation."

"Into what?" Jillian White, a nurse, asked.

"We can't say at this time but rest assured that as soon

as we have what we need, the quarantine will be lifted."

"And how long will that take?" Jenna asked. "We have families, kids that are expecting us home."

"We understand that and can appreciate the inconvenience but it's for your safety and theirs that we do this."

Summers rose to his feet. "Safety? Let me go out on a limb here and you tell me if I'm off base. You show up here in hazmat suits, you quarantine this place, tell us this is a matter of national security and say that none of us can leave because it's for the safety of our families. We are dealing with some kind of pandemic, aren't we? That's why you're here."

"I'm a USAMRIID virologist, we are investing an outbreak. That's all I can tell you. And like with any outbreak we have to take measures to ensure the safety of the general public. We are not doing this to ruin your day."

"And yet you are," Trish said. "This is bullshit!"

The colonel eyed Trish through narrowed eyes. Jenna

placed a hand on hers to try and keep her calm. She knew there was no point in them getting upset by this. The military personnel were following protocol, that's all. Not telling them what the outbreak was, was to be expected.

* * *

Nick's stomach dropped as the door flew open, then relaxed when he saw it was Callie Madison. "Callie?" She closed the door behind her but not before peering out. Nick dropped down off the ladder and made his way over. "How did you get out?"

"I left just after you two did but saw you duck into the washroom. I went into the science lab and stayed in the resources room until it was quiet. I came out and saw you two darting in and out of rooms but I couldn't catch up until now. What are you doing?"

He brought her up to speed.

"Did you see what they are doing to them?" Devan asked.

She nodded. "They are all sitting in the gymnasium under armed guard. The teachers are doing roll call. What the hell is going on?"

"There's no time to discuss that now, we need to get out."

"And go where?"

"My father is waiting for us at Coffield Park."

"And then where he's taking you?" she asked.

Devan walked over to the ladder, getting ready to head up. "Who knows but it's better than being stuck here. You coming or not?"

She nodded and all three of them ascended the rusted ladder. At the top, Devan popped the hatch open and they crawled onto a gravel roof, keeping low. The school itself was divided into sections, some areas had slanted roofs and others were flat. Nick closed the hatch behind them and they jogged over to the edge of the building on the east side and looked out. There had to have been ten military vehicles positioned in various spots around the school grounds. Soldiers were walking the perimeter of the school while others were going in and out.

"We don't stand a chance," Callie said.

Nick darted over to the west side which faced Gonzales Street. That also had vehicles. The south side was the same on Lincoln Street, which left only the north end. They hopped down about six feet onto an adjoining roof, crossed over and jumped to a slanted metal roof and made their way to the north side. That side was different. There were a few military trucks parked close to the building but nowhere as many as the other three sides.

Devan dropped down to his knees and put his head in his hands.

"We aren't getting off, are we?"

Nick didn't reply, instead he was trying to gauge the distance between the school building and the cafeteria which was a separate area divided by a parking lot. It had to have been about twenty to thirty yards. If they could get to it, they stood a chance of making it over to Murphy Street and heading west towards the park.

"Look, this isn't going to be easy and there is a good chance we'll be spotted but I'd rather take my chances trying to get the hell out of here than give myself up.

What do you say?"

Devan grimaced.

Callie was the first to respond. "What's the plan?"

Chapter 8

It was a roadblock. Why the hell had they set up a roadblock in Alpine? Brody had attempted multiple times to reach other officers back in Marfa on the radio but without success before he made the decision to continue on.

"Leave this to me," Gottman said. "There is probably a very good reason for all of this. It's possible they have an escaped convict. It wouldn't be the first time they have got the National Guard involved."

He was right.

Brody veered off the hard shoulder and continued on getting closer to the checkpoint. There was a large fire engine with its lights flashing cutting off a portion of the road, as well as a military truck and two cop cars. As they got closer two soldiers wearing hazmat suits stepped forward with rifles at the ready. Brody brought his truck to a crawl and lowered the window.

"Where you coming from?" they asked.

"We were south of Marfa viewing point on the Mitchell Flat recovering a body."

Gottman hopped out and the soldiers raised their rifles. "Get back inside the vehicle," one of them yelled.

"I'm a cop with Alpine." He gestured towards the officers that were about a hundred yards away. "These officers will vouch for that." He also turned his arm to show them the patch on his shoulder. "This is the chief of police from Marfa," he said. "We're just transporting back a body related to an open case. You want to tell me what's going on?"

"Hold tight," the soldier said getting on his radio and walking a short distance away. Brody gripped the steering wheel tight and felt uncomfortable as the other soldier kept his weapon trained on him. There was no escaped convict. They would have said it and waved them on in. Something wasn't right. The soldier who was on the radio returned and waved them on in. Gottman hopped back in with a smile on his face. "Told you. They just needed to speak to the right person."

Although Brody had his reservations about heading into town, until he could speak to the chief of Alpine, he wouldn't have a clear picture of what was happening. The fire truck reversed, allowing them room to pass through. As they drove on, Gottman gave a nod to his fellow officers. He might have felt comfortable with this situation but Brody sure as hell didn't.

* * *

Emerick Jones sat in the idling Chevy Blazer just on the outskirts of Coffield Park near the baseball diamond, waiting for his son. His heart ached recalling all the years he'd spent bringing his kid out here and watching him play. That was until he reached his teen years, and his mother had taken off with some other guy, leaving Emerick to raise him. It had caused him a great deal of pain to lose her but what hurt worse was seeing Devan in pain. Nowadays he acted as if it didn't affect him but it did. He just kept it bottled up inside. Emerick kept staring at his phone on the dashboard expecting it to buzz with a text while Angela kept watch on the road ahead and behind them.

"They've locked down the hospital in Alpine and now the school in Marfa. Why isn't anyone reporting this online? They might have been able to get away with this back in the '80s but..." He scooped up his phone and noticed the Internet had stopped working. "Oh, c'mon!" he yelled. "Angela, check your phone. Is the Internet working for you?"

She fished it out of her pocket and shook her head. "And I'm also not getting any signal either."

"What?"

He looked back down at his and sure enough the bars were gone. It didn't take a rocket scientist to see what was going on. The military had shut down the Internet and all communication lines. Whatever shit they were pulling, they were making sure that no one was going to spread the word which also told him that whatever he'd seen earlier was perhaps isolated to Marfa and Alpine.

His nerves were starting to get the better of him.

"We might not be out of the woods yet. I just saw a military truck pass by West Lincoln Street. We can't stay out here too much longer."

"We aren't a threat."

"They're looking for us. Remember?"

He nodded. He'd put the incident on the street to the back of his mind and hadn't thought of anything else except getting his son out of harm's way. It also wasn't like they could conceal their vehicle behind trees. Coffield Park was an open space with a few shady areas where trees were dotted. It was probably the greenest area inside of Marfa's town limits. Tourists and locals alike would go there to unwind. It was common to see people walking, running or playing with kids in the park. It didn't offer much but Marfa residents weren't exactly high-maintenance individuals.

"Listen, what happens if he doesn't show?"

"Then I go find him. I'm not leaving him."

"Emerick. If this is some kind of imposition of martial law, and people are being rounded up and shipped off to

FEMA camps, I'm not putting myself in that. My mother is in an Alpine nursing home. I need to make sure that she's okay."

"First, we're not heading to Alpine. You think it's any better there? Second, I hardly think FEMA is involved in this."

"You heard it yourself from our guest the other night."

"The guy was a conspiracy nut ranting about U.S. citizens being imprisoned for the purpose of extermination as part of a New World Order, Angela. I think we can take what he said with a grain of salt."

"Most consider you a conspiracy nut."

"Just because it's a part of our weekly show, doesn't mean I agree with it." He reached for a pack of smokes and tapped one out before lighting it. His hand was still shaking from nerves. He brought the window down and blew gray smoke out the corner of his mouth. "It's all about numbers. We have to appeal to the masses, we can't just run a regular radio show. That shit doesn't fly nowadays. You have to have your hand in everything."

He took another hit on his cigarette. "Besides, if they've shut off the communication and Internet in both towns, I hardly think they are going to cart us all off to a concentration camp. This is the concentration camp. They only need to set up borders, post police and military at every exit out of town and they have us hedged in like rats in a science lab experiment."

She nodded and tapped her fingers against her leg.

Emerick had known Angela for over fifteen years. In all that time she'd never got married, had a kid or shown any sign of settling down. Some even thought she was a lesbian because she trimmed her hair short and was only ever seen with women in bars. But he didn't buy it. There was more to her story but he'd never really got into it with her. "Why don't you date guys?"

"What?" she said flashing him a glance, confused by the question.

"Guys. Dating. I never hear you talking about them."

She shrugged. "I guess I just haven't got around to it."

"But don't you feel alone?"

"I guess. I mean, yeah, of course. I have nights where I wish someone was there when I came home but I have a lot of good friends."

"Females."

She got this smile on her face.

"Not you as well."

"Well you have to admit, Angela, it's kind of odd. Even Suzie Foster has a man, and she's a real hag. You're much better looking than her."

"Well thank you. Though I'm not sure if I should take that as a compliment or an insult." She scoffed looking back at out the window.

"I'm just saying, a little bit of a makeover and you really could turn heads."

"Emerick."

"What?"

"Shut the hell up."

* * *

Back at the high school, Nick had watched the soldiers go in and out of the north entrance. No matter how they did this, there was a good chance they'd be caught. "Listen to me. If any one of us gets caught, the others don't stop. Just keep going. I mean that. If they grab me you keep going."

"I intend to," Devan said with a smile on his face. One of the military trucks was parked close to the building, close enough that if they made their way down a thick drainpipe at the side they could launch themselves on top of the canvas roof. From there they would slide down, hide beneath it and time their mad dash to the cafeteria building. Nick was the first to go down. Devan and Callie watched him as he descended and dropped down to the truck. When he hit the top, it gave way a little then bounced like a soft bed. He waited there flat on his face for a minute or two before giving them the thumbs-up. Callie was next. Once she landed, Devan wasn't that far behind.

As he was scaling down the pipe, Nick heard several soldiers talking to one another. They emerged from a side door. He couldn't shout, or even whistle, all he could do was grit his teeth and hope to God Devan heard them.

"We're leaving in fifteen to collect supplies. The colonel wants to keep them here until FEMA runs its tests on the kids."

Nick eyed them, then Devan. Fortunately Devan had heard them and had frozen in place. He was literally above their heads, clutching hold of the black pipe. If they looked up they would spot him. One of them took out a cigarette and lit it. "That kid who was shot. I didn't sign up for that."

"The day you entered boot camp you signed away your rights. Now just do your job and shut up."

Another soldier joined them outside to have a smoke. All any of them could do was remain still and quiet and hope to God they went back inside. If they stayed outside, it was over. Nick looked at Devan and stared back and got this smile on his face, the same kind he got when he was about to do something real stupid.

"Hey assholes!" Devan yelled.

Nick's jaw dropped as he watched Devan scale back up

the pipe like a monkey. The soldiers looked up and two of them rushed inside while the other attempted to scale up the pipe. That was their cue. As much as Nick didn't want to leave him there, they had no choice. He knew what he'd done. He'd given himself up so they could escape as the chances of them being able to run across that parking lot without being spotted were slim to none. Nick nudged Callie and they climbed over the side out of view of the soldier and dropped to the ground. They rolled underneath for a second just to reassess the situation. One of the soldiers had now scaled up the pipe, and they could hear him shouting for Devan to stop. They knew it was now or never. Quickly they scrambled out and sprinted across the lot, slipped down the side of the cafeteria, entered Murphy Street and began running west as fast as they could. They would have to go three blocks before they could go south to Coffield Park.

Nick clutched Callie's hand as they dashed through house yards and took a shortcut to get to the park. All the while Nick kept looking over his shoulder, expecting to be pursued by cops or soldiers, but no one followed them.

He could only hope that Devan got away.

* * *

Brody and Gottman arrived at the Alpine City Police Department on Sul Ross Avenue to find even more military vehicles on site. Brody parked in front of a low-slung building next to a black-and-white. He only had one goal in mind and that was to speak to Chief Westlake. They entered the building which was absent of all police officers barring two, one at the front desk and another on the phone. It wasn't a large department and only had eleven officers for a town of six thousand.

"Hey Maise, the chief in?" Gottman asked the gal at the front desk. She thumbed over her shoulder and put her head down. Gottman led the way taking them through a series of corridors down to a large office at the corner of the building. He knocked once before opening the door. Inside was Chief Paul Westlake, and across from him was a large, overbearing man dressed in full military regalia.

"Ah, Gottman, come in."

"Hi Paul," Brody said as he walked in. He eyed the military bigwig and closed the door behind him. "We were hoping to speak with you in private."

"I was just about to leave," the stranger said, rising from his chair, putting his cap on and turning to Westlake. "Remember what I said."

"Understood," Westlake replied.

"Gentlemen," the stranger said before leaving.

As soon as the door was closed, Gottman unleashed. "Chief, what the hell is going on?"

He leaned back in his seat. "It's out of my hands. They are here to stay until they have investigated an outbreak."

"An outbreak?" Brody asked.

"That's what he said."

"And who was that?"

"Major Tim Brown from the USAMRIID."

"The what?" Gottman spluttered.

"The United States Army Medical Research Institute of Infectious Diseases."

Both of them stared back at him with a look of shock.

"Um, Brody, your wife is at the hospital and they've quarantined it. They are also preventing anyone from leaving the town until they have isolated, and tested each and every resident."

"But my son is back in Marfa."

"I'm sorry."

Brody regretted entering now. He should have figured this was going to happen. What other reason would they have checkpoints at the exit of the town? He pulled out his phone and tried to make a few calls, one to his son and the other to Jenna.

"Don't bother. They've shut it down."

He glanced up at Westlake and then looked at his phone.

There was no signal.

Chapter 9

He'd given those bastards one hell of a run for their money. They certainly earned their wages that afternoon. Although Devan was pissed that he hadn't managed to escape with the others, he felt a deep sense of satisfaction knowing that he'd stuck his neck out on the line. He felt like a real American hero, the kind his grandfather used to talk about. He'd told him countless stories of what it was like in Vietnam and some of the heroic acts of soldiers. Well, all that heroism, and puffed-up attitude, soon vanished when they nabbed him running across the football field. Yep, he'd managed to actually outrun the idiot who chased him on the roof, then zip by four more soldiers on the ground and another two on his way over to the field. Had it not been for the rubber bullet that hit him in the shoulder he was positive he would have escaped.

Now he found himself chewing grass, and a mouthful

of dirt. The pain was excruciating. He was sure they'd shot him for real. Without knowing what it felt like to be shot, he could only assume the worst. Yet before he could tell if there was any blood, two of them piled on top of him and one dug a knee into his back while the other zip tied him.

"That was a stupid move, kid."

"Yeah, but I outran you assholes. Uncle Sam would be real disappointed."

"Shut the hell up and get up."

"And to think they spend thousands of dollars on training you buffoons, only to get outrun by a seventeen-year-old." Devan laughed in between wincing in pain as they strong-armed him to his feet and forced him back to the school. One of them got on the radio.

"We got him." The soldier turned to him. "Any others out here?"

He shook his head. "Nope, just me."

Devan looked off towards the cafeteria, wondering where they were now. He thought about his father and hoped he wouldn't do anything stupid. This wasn't like the end of the world. It was a bump in the road, a mere hurdle that he would again jump over. There was no chance in hell they were keeping him locked hp.

Pushed on, he grimaced in pain and one of the soldiers told him to stop whining like a bitch. "It was just a rubber bullet. You were lucky we didn't shoot you with the real thing."

"Yeah. Like the guy you shot earlier."

"That was a rubber bullet, asshole."

"Yeah, whatever helps you sleep at night," Devan muttered.

They led him back through a set of double doors, down a hallway and into the gymnasium. That's when he got a better view of the situation. All the students had been crammed in there, most had filled up the bleachers, the rest were sitting on their butts while soldiers dotted around the room kept their rifles trained on them. He groaned inwardly. This wasn't going to be as easy as he thought.

They cut his zip tie and shoved him to the ground.

"Hey!" Mr. Harper said, sticking up for him. His protest was quickly silenced with a rifle barrel to his face. All he could do now was hope for the best but expect the worst.

* * *

Out of breath, Nick and Callie made their way down Mesa Street, taking cover every so often behind vehicles as military trucks rolled by. The place was swarming with them. After a few more minutes of running, they spotted Devan's father's Chevy. He'd parked it just off the road, up the side of the baseball diamond. Double-timing it they hurried over, startling Emerick and Angela as they came up behind the truck and slammed into it.

"Nick. Thank God. I thought you…" Emerick looked out his window and scanned the terrain behind them. "Where is Devan?"

Still trying to get his breath, Nick hopped in and Angela passed him a bottle of water.

"Nick!"

"Emerick, give them a second to catch their breaths."

Nick chugged down the water like he was putting out an internal fire, and then handed it to Callie who did the same. After, he told him. It was like watching a balloon lose all its air. Emerick's shoulder dropped and he got this faraway look in his eyes. "If he hadn't done that there was a chance we wouldn't have got away."

"Yeah. That's my boy."

"What's going on?" Callie asked, hoping they might have answers.

"That's what we'd like to know. Did you see anything, hear anything at the school?" Angela said, filling in for Emerick who looked too distraught to speak.

"Nothing," she replied.

"I heard something," Nick chimed in. All of them looked at him. "I mean besides gunshots, I heard one of the soldiers say that they were keeping everyone at the school until FEMA ran tests on them. One of them also mentioned killing a student. I don't know if there is any truth to that but I did hear a gunshot."

Angela squeezed the bridge of her nose. "Oh my God, this can't be happening. FEMA? What the hell are they doing in Marfa?"

Emerick ran two hands over his face. "It's pretty obvious. This has to be some kind of outbreak. Tests. FEMA. Soldiers taking away people who came in contact with Tim on the road. We're looking at something infectious."

"Like the flu?"

He shook his head. "No, something is different about this." He turned in his seat. "Nick, did any of the students act differently? Out of character?"

Before he could reply, Callie piped up. "Well, yeah, Toby Winters before he..." she trailed off and then continued. "He was acting strange like he was in a dazed state or frozen almost. Then when I clicked my fingers near him he acted as if he was scared. I mean really scared."

"That was before he jumped off the building," Nick said.

"Jumped off the school?" Angela asked.

He nodded. "He wasn't the only one. There was some kid who cut off his hand in the bleachers. He did it on purpose. I mean, who the hell does that kind of shit?"

"People infected with something, or suffering from something." Emerick jammed the gearstick into gear.

"Where we heading?" Nick asked

"To my place. I need to collect some supplies, and gear up."

Nick glanced at Callie, fearing the worst.

* * *

Daniel Sorenson had worked for the CDC for close to nine years as an epidemiologist and in all his time investigating diseases, he'd never seen anything like this. The report had been sent over by Colonel Lynch twelve hours ago and he'd gone over with it a fine-tooth comb, reading the study that was done on the now deceased soldiers and the scientists' theories on the breach. Similar to the CDC, the USAMRIID ran its own experiments with different virus strains, and although they said they were in compliance with the CDC and the WHO, he knew better. The CDC was only called in when they had screwed up, and this was a major one.

Late last night he'd kissed his wife of twenty-six years goodbye and caught a red-eye flight out of Chicago. Fortunately he didn't have any kids so he only had his wife to worry about. When he touched down at Midland Airport in Texas he was so exhausted he put his head down for a couple of hours in the back of a cab on the journey into Alpine. Even though the military had stressed the urgency of the matter, he needed to be awake enough to be able to handle it, and as of late he hadn't been getting much sleep due to a new virus that the CDC was studying that had the potential to wipe out millions if it wasn't properly stored or escaped the lab. He thought back to the accidental exposure of dozens of workers to anthrax in 2014 and some of the protocols that were not followed by lab workers. It was at that time he recalled vials of deadly smallpox being found in cardboard boxes in an unsecured refrigerator at a campus in Bethesda,

Maryland. It was proof of how easily something so deadly could get out of hand.

Now arriving in Alpine he could tell from the immense military presence that this was more serious than he'd anticipated. He'd been told to head to the hospital and to be ready to begin testing subjects. Colonel Lynch wasn't even there to greet him when he arrived. He was escorted through a series of corridors that had been cleared of patients and led into an onsite lab where they had arranged to have everything he needed. Several army doctors and pathologists were on hand as were soldiers to watch over them for their own protection.

It was one thing to read about the problem in a report, another to see a live test subject, one that had been exposed to the virus. While they had shared their theories on how it had escaped the lab, no one was any closer to understanding how it had spread from one person to the next because when their test had been conducted on the nine soldiers, each of them had been injected with the sample. Still, his job wasn't to figure out how it had transferred, instead his task was to find a cure, and find out if anyone was immune to it.

It was an arduous task that he thought he was up to dealing with until two soldiers brought in the first patient infected with what they were calling amygdala syndrome. The USAMRIID referred to it as that, as it affected the specific part of the brain that tackled the fight-or-flight survival instinct in humans. It was associated with many responses in the human body, specifically fear, arousal, autonomic responses, emotional, hormonal and even memory. Under the right conditions the amygdala would work to a person's advantage but if a disease affected it, the repercussions could be devastating.

The dark-haired, five-foot-four woman with ocean-blue eyes fought the soldiers every step of the way as they wrestled to bring her in. Once she was restrained to a chair for general observation, he took her through a series of blood, saliva, visual and hearing tests while he spoke into his phone to record what he was seeing.

All he'd been told was that she was fine twelve hours

ago.

"On the surface, it appears she is suffering from a severe form of Urbach-Wiethe disease. There is a thickening of the skin and mucous membranes but also redness to the eyes. Would like to see what she looked like twelve hours ago."

Once he had conducted his observations, he handed her off to another doctor who would perform a brain scan that would allow them to get a better idea of what was happening. All the military had said was they were working on a new form of drug that would control fear and anxiety. And while the reports of incidents both within the military and in the public had demonstrated that people were showing signs of fearlessness, there was also an increase in anger. It was almost like they were going through a metamorphosis, which was causing subjects to become unstable. The question was, what kind of change was occurring and why had the drug failed?

Out of the nine soldiers who were dead, six had died from gunshot wounds from the military trying to control them, the other three had died of natural causes. Sorenson looked at the report again. Blood seeped from eyes, nose and ears, and after seventy-two hours, their hearts stopped from what they could determine was the release of adrenaline in their system. Essentially, causing a cardiac arrest.

Eight more patients were brought in, each one with different symptoms and reactions to him. Some reared back from him in a petrified state, others looked frozen, and others were belligerent, aggressive and trying to lash out.

As the day wore on he began to see some of the doctors and nurses in the hospital, those who had treated patients but weren't exhibiting any signs of infection.

They next patient was a nurse. He glanced down at the clipboard in front of him and looked at her. She was a good-looking woman, five-six in stature, athletic, early forties, shoulder-length dark hair, oval face with green eyes. Unlike the last one she was compliant and dressed in scrubs.

"Jenna Jackson?"

"That's right," she said yanking her arm away from an officer and then telling him she could take a seat by herself.

"You work here at the hospital."

"Worked. Yes. Until the military strong-armed their way in."

"You've been in contact with several test subjects who are exhibiting flu-like symptoms: headaches, cough, runny nose, watery eyes, fever. Yes?"

"I'm a nurse, what do you think?"

He looked up from his clipboard and smiled. He understood why she was pissed. He would be if he were in the same position. The military would have told them very little about the disease, which would have led to frustration, confusion and eventually anger. He brought out a light and shone it in her eyes. "That's good. Thank you," he said, acknowledging that she was behaving well. "I was looking through the list of patients you have seen over the past twenty-four hours, two of them are exhibiting symptoms and yet you don't appear to be any worse for wear. You're either lucky or you might be of further use."

"Further use?"

He studied her expression. Instead of answering that he said, "We want to run some blood tests, a quick MRI scan, and you should be good to go back."

"What kind of virus are you looking at?" she asked as he turned his back to jot down a few notes.

"The kind that requires shutting down an entire town," he said. It wasn't his position to explain to her what was happening. The whole project was shrouded in secrecy and he reported to the CDC and Lynch, that was it. Yet on the other hand, he wanted her to understand that it wasn't just the hospital that had been quarantined. At the bare minimum he could offer her that kind of information.

* * *

Four hours later, Colonel Lynch was getting an update from one of the soldiers on the situation inside the town when Sorenson approached her. "A moment of your time."

"Certainly." She turned back to the soldier and told him to keep her informed of any changes. As it stood, things were quiet at each of the checkpoints and locals were taking it all in stride but that wouldn't last. If they didn't get on top of this fast, determine who was infected and isolate them, they would have a war on their hands. Citizens wouldn't put up with being held prisoner in their own town without just cause, and as they couldn't say much the situation had the potential to get volatile.

Lynch jerked her head towards an empty office and Sorenson followed her in.

"Close the door behind you."

She took a seat and pulled in close to the desk.

"How have the tests been coming along?"

"Slow. You are aware of how many patients and staff are in this place?"

"What have been the results so far?" she asked without answering his question. She wasn't going to get into it with him. They had a job to do and that was it.

"Based on the blood samples taken from the deceased soldiers we've been able to compare that with those here and determine who is and who isn't infected but again it's a slow process to get through everyone. It appears there are signs of it showing in the bloodstream within the first few hours of infection, and by the twelve-hour mark you are looking at external signs — flu-like symptoms, thickening of skin and mucus etcetera. Strangely enough I have managed to find six people who are showing signs of infection in the blood but aren't showing any symptoms, which could just mean they are immune. I won't know without at least another twenty-four hours of observation."

Lynch nodded. "Well that's at least promising. And if they are immune?"

"We would go about making an antivirus." He paused and stared at her. "Colonel, may I speak straight with you?"

"Feel free," she replied leaning back in her seat.

"What is going to happen to those who are infected?"

"They will be isolated until they die."

"And what of those in the town? The ones we aren't going to be able to test? People who might be infected. You can't honestly think that the military can hold all of them with those checkpoints."

"Daniel, isn't it?"

"Yes."

"Daniel, you stick to running tests and leave the rest to us. This isn't our first rodeo and I doubt it will be our last."

Chapter 10

Sergio and Lars had managed to elude the soldiers using ATVs. It took them a good fifty minutes to arrive at Viola's burial site. The plan was to dig up her body, and haul her carcass up to the mountains where they could find a more discreet and less obvious final resting place. He couldn't have anyone stumbling across it. His DNA was on her and that's what had given him cause for worry over the past five days. What if someone found her? What if they managed to get him on DNA? Why hadn't he worn gloves? He'd thought of everything else except that. He hopped off the bike and turned on a bright flashlight. Lars arrived a minute after him. He killed the engine and pulled down his American flag bandanna that was covering the lower half of his face.

"Did you see how many soldiers there were?" Lars asked.

"Don't worry about that and just give me a hand."

They trudged down into the valley, scanning the terrain and washing the light over the landscape. As it was now nighttime it was harder to locate her but he'd set down a reflector nestled into the rocks to use as a guide just in case he had to come back at night. He kept raking the flashlight until he saw it glimmer.

"There we go. Up ahead."

"Sergio, I don't like this. Why don't you just get out of town? Go visit your brother in Mexico."

"Yeah, and how that's going to look? Hell no, that cow might have screwed up my life while she was alive but she's not doing it now she's dead. I'm staying put."

"I'm just saying."

"Why, you thinking of leaving?"

"It's crossed my mind," Lars replied. "I just want to put this all behind me."

"And we are. Tonight we'll bury her and no one will find her."

"What about the town?"

"What about it?" Sergio said without looking at him

and trudging on.

"If the military is stopping people, maybe we should just lay low for a while. Head up to El Paso. My sister is up there and we can spend a few weeks kicking back."

"Be my guest. I'm not leaving. I don't have the time to—" Sergio suddenly went quiet. "Shit. Shit. Shit!" he cried out, his voice getting louder by the second. He sprinted forward to the area where they'd buried Viola only to find a hole in the ground. "No. No. This can't be right. She was right here."

"Are you sure this is the hole?" Lars asked scanning the dark landscape. "I mean it's dark out here. Perhaps you got it wrong."

"I know this is." Sergio dropped down to his knees and began digging with his hands, throwing back large amounts of loose desert sand. "She was right here. I know it."

"Sergio," Lars said shining his light a few feet away. "There are boot prints leading in and out of this place." Sergio scrambled up and followed the path up and out of the valley, his mind rushing with thoughts of the worst. What if it was the cops? Would they come searching for him? No. It would take them time to do an autopsy but…he trailed off thinking about all the scenarios. It only ended one way and that was with them finding his DNA and then wanting to take a swab.

"I said we shouldn't have buried her here."

Sergio spun around, rage getting the better of him. He grabbed Lars and shook him like a rag doll. "This is your fault."

"Mine?"

"I wanted to head out here earlier this week but you wouldn't go."

"I had work. I'm sorry my life prevented you from covering your tracks to a murder but maybe you shouldn't have killed her in the first place."

"What?"

"She hadn't done anything wrong, Sergio."

"She was going to cheat on me. She was cheating on me."

"You're deluded, man."

Sergio pushed him away and took out his Glock and aimed at him. "What's that? Huh? What did you say?" He pressed the gun against the side of his head and dared him to say another word. Lars remained quiet. Just as he thought, all mouth and no action. Seeing Lars wasn't going to be a problem he pulled the piece away from his head and continued on trudging up a steep incline following the tracks.

"What if it is the cops?" Lars asked.

"If they found her today, I hardly think they are going to have a chance to do an autopsy, with what's going on in the town and all. So we have a window of opportunity."

He didn't need to explain to him what he meant by that, he knew.

Sergio wasn't going down for this.

* * *

Devan's father lived in a dated shack at the far end of North Gonzales Street. It was literally on the perimeter of the town. Beyond that was the desert plains, nothing but miles of grit, dust and sand for as far as the eye could see. After the sun had set, Emerick had driven with his lights off to avoid military patrolling the streets. Before Devan's mother had run off with some sleaze ball she'd met in a bar in Marfa, they'd lived in a fairly decent neighborhood — North Gonzales didn't even come close. On either side of the road were trailers. Barring one modern adobe-style house close to Emerick's, the whole neighborhood looked like a run-down trailer park. It was cheap, and his father had bought the place after some old-timer passed away and the trailer sat on the market for the better part of a year.

Emerick parked the Chevy under a carport beside a busted-up Jeep Wrangler that had the rear wheels off. It was a work in progress, something that he was planning on passing down to Devan, at least that's what he said but he'd never really got around to doing anything except take the wheels off. It was quiet when they got out. A glow of yellow emanated from the neighbor's trailer across the road as Emerick fumbled with the keys before letting them inside.

Nick had been there countless times over the past six years. It always had this unusual dank smell to the place because Devan's old man would smoke weed. It was for his back, Emerick would say but that was bull crap, he just enjoyed getting high.

Inside it wasn't fancy. A worn brown leather couch set back against the far wall, a thin coffee table, one IKEA chair that they'd picked up at a yard sale and a round table in the kitchen. The counters were dated, the linoleum flooring warped, and the paint was peeling but it was home and better than being on the streets. Emerick tossed his keys into a brass holder to his right as he entered and made a beeline for the fridge. He peered inside, flooding the room with light before Angela turned on the main switch. Emerick took out a beer and cracked it open, chugging it back fast before crushing the can and tossing it into the trash.

Angela slumped down on the couch and put her head

in her hands. Callie stood there looking out of place. Nick followed Emerick down the hall into the bedroom where he rooted through his closet and pulled out a duffel bag. His bedroom was a mess. It was just a mattress on the floor with a duvet cover thrown on top, and two pillows. Covering the single window was an American flag, and at the far end of his bed was a sofa. Beside his bed was a waste paper basket full of used tissues, and a half-open car magazine just visible beneath a pile of clothes. He began tossing in clothes haphazardly, and slipped by him only to return with toiletries. All the while he was muttering to himself as if trying to keep track of what he was there to do.

"I knew a day like this would come," Emerick said.

"I've been telling you that for years," Angela replied from in the living room

Emerick reached under his bed and pulled out a small black case, he unlocked it and inside was a Glock 19. He then got down real low and reached under and retrieved two boxes of ammo. He stuffed all of it inside his duffel bag, zipped it up and headed back into the kitchen. Emerick dropped the bag and continued on through to another area. Nick heard him jangle some keys and then a moment later he emerged holding a Winchester rifle.

"Holy crap, Emerick, we aren't going to war," Angela said.

"You heard what Nick said. If these soldiers are killing people, the line in the sand has been crossed."

"Look, maybe we should stay here the night," Callie said. "Things might be better in the morning."

"Better? Better!" he bellowed.

"Emerick," Nick said noticing that he was scaring Callie.

"It's not going to be better only worse. If we don't move now and use the night as cover, we don't stand a chance tomorrow."

"And what's your plan, huh?" Callie asked.

"We're heading to Alpine," Nick said. "To speak to my father." Angela nodded in agreement thinking of her mother in the retirement home.

170

"I didn't say we were going there," Emerick said as he brushed past him and scooped up the bag and began filling it with bottles of water and several cans of food.

"But—" Nick said before Emerick cut him off.

"My main concern is Devan. Once I have him back, we're getting out of here."

Nick crossed the room and pointed towards where he imagined the school would be in relation to the trailer. "Devan is locked up, under the watchful eyes of soldiers. What are you going to do, go Rambo on them?"

"I'll figure it out when I get there."

"Don't be stupid, Emerick," Angela said rising to her feet. Nick was glad to have her there as a voice of reason as right then he wasn't thinking clearly. He was being driven by the pain of losing his kid. "You go charging in there, you're only going to get yourself in trouble. Hell, they might even shoot you. You want that?"

Emerick looked down at the ground as if he was contemplating. He opened his mouth to say something when they heard a commotion outside. It sounded like someone screaming. Emerick shot over to the window and pulled back the drapes to see. Again, another scream.

"What the hell?" Emerick muttered.

"What's going on?" Angela said.

"Stay here," he said grabbing up his rifle and heading for the door. Nick wasn't far behind. Emerick glanced at him but for whatever reason chose not to stop him. They headed out into the night. Emerick told Nick to stay behind him. "If I tell you go to run back, you do it and lock those doors. You understand?"

He nodded. As they came around the corner of his trailer, in the middle of the road was a man without a shirt, or socks, straddling what appeared to be an unconscious man.

"Gary?" Emerick said. No response. "Gary?"

The man's head turned and light from a floodlight revealed the true horror. Gripped in his hand was a 10-inch carving knife, and all down the front of Gary's chest was blood. His victim, an elderly man in his seventies, had a massive gash on his throat and multiple stab wounds to his chest. Gary got up and without saying a word started heading towards them.

"Now Gary. Stay back," Emerick said, beginning to raise his rifle.

Gary ignored the request and charged forward, his eyes wild and the knife raised in the air. Emerick didn't hesitate. A crack echoed, followed by another and Gary hit the ground. They stood there in silence and shock.

Nick was the first one to get close but he didn't go too close.

"Holy shit," he muttered. "That really happened."

It was like something out of a movie. He couldn't believe what he was seeing. "We need to call the ambulance."

"No ambulance is coming," Emerick said. "Only the military."

Several neighbors came out and stared, some placed hands over their mouths. Emerick walked over to a trailer across the road. "Emily?" he called out but there was no answer. He approached the door and used the end of the gun barrel to pull the screen door open. Nick could see him out the corner of his eye.

"Emily?"

He turned his head and saw Emerick push the door open, then he stumbled back. "Dear God."

"What is it?" Nick asked.

"We need to go."

"What?"

"Now."

Emerick came down a few wooden steps and made his way back.

Nick was frozen in place unable to believe what he'd just witnessed. He'd seen people killed on TV but this was the real deal.

"Nick. We need to go. Now!"

He backed up slowly then broke into a jog hurrying back to the trailer.

* * *

Back in Alpine, Brody had been trying to get an update on the situation at the hospital. Even though he and Jenna weren't on good terms, he cared for her dearly and this whole event had driven that home even more so.

"What do you mean?"

"I'm sorry, sir, no one goes in or out. Strict orders."

Brody pointed to the main doors. "But I'm a cop. My wife is in there."

"I'm sorry, sir. No exceptions."

Gottman raised a hand to the soldier. "It's all good. We'll wait until the quarantine's lifted. C'mon, chief." He guided him away and they returned to Brody's truck. As soon as they were inside, Gottman said, "I know you want to see her but we got to face reality here. If there is some kind of pandemic, do you really want to go in there and expose yourself to that?"

Brody gripped the steering wheel tight and glanced at the hospital.

"I mean, I thought things between you and her were over?"

"I never said that."

Gottman groaned and ran a hand over his face while

looking out the window. "Look, you would need some kind of respirator and goggles if you went in there. I think I know how to get some."

Brody shot him a sideways glance and Gottman's lip curled up at the corner. Gottman had always been a wild card. How he had ever made it through police academy was anyone's guess. It came as no surprise to Brody when he told him what he had in mind.

"Are you kidding?"

"How bad do you want to get in there?" Gottman asked.

"You know they could throw our asses in jail for that."

"I'd like to see them try."

Brody frowned. "Why do you want to stick your neck out for me? I know you wanted this position."

"I did. You're right. I was pissed you got selected over me but that was then. I've come to realize that you have to put up with a lot more shit than I do, and let's face it, you don't get paid much more than us."

"Ah, you would be surprised at the Christmas bonus,"

Brody replied.

"Asshole," Gottman said before laughing. Brody backed out of the lot and onto Fort Davis Highway. Before heading south he looked towards the north where another checkpoint was stationed. A big rig had been moved across the road, and it appeared from looking into the distance that the entrance points to Alpine weren't the only areas they were beginning to patrol. He saw several Humvees and an M117 Guardian roaming the perimeter of the town, shining a large spotlight across the homes. He drove south back into town and continued on Highway 118 following Gottman's directions.

"Take a left onto 223."

"But there isn't much out here."

"That's right but for where we're going it will get us there."

"Is that where you went earlier?"

"No, I went to check on my brother. I then took a browse around the town to see where soldiers were stationed. For the most part they are focused on the main stretch, the roads in and out, the university, and around the perimeter, though they aren't doing a good job with that. I saw several people managed to get out on dirt bikes."

"Amateurs," Brody said.

They continued on until he veered onto I-90 and headed east. "You taking us out of town?"

"No, but I saw some of their troops parked by Penny's Diner. I guess they're taking advantage of our good ol' home-style cooking."

"And?"

"Just follow my lead. Trust me," Gottman said.

"That's what I'm worried about."

They veered into the lot outside across from the Oak Tree Inn and Gottman told him to wait while he went inside. Brody stayed in the vehicle as it idled and looked through the windows at some of the patrons who were either blissfully unaware or too scared to do anything but go with the flow.

Penny's Diner was what some might have labeled a

greasy spoon hellhole on the side of the road, but to locals it was a slice of home. Brody had taken Nick there countless times for breakfast while visiting him. The food was good. The prices were reasonable and staff were friendly. On the outside it looked like a house of mirrors with warped-looking steel that stretched for twenty yards, and gave you the impression that you were entering a steel works, but looks could be deceiving. Inside it was narrow, like a train car, and had a retro feel to it with tables along the wall and shiny stools dotted along the breakfast counter. The floors were checkered in black and white and there was a Victorian style to the ceiling.

Brody observed the military truck in the lot and waited.

Several minutes went by before Gottman reappeared followed by two soldiers. He was acting all theatrical, waving his arms around and pointing in a direction heading out of town. He broke away from the soldiers while they hurried to their truck. Gottman jumped in. "Okay, head out, they're going to follow us."

"What did you tell them?" Brody asked.

"That I had got wind of a group of people who were looking to leave town tonight, and one of them was showing symptoms of the flu."

"They're going to radio for backup, you do know that?"

"No time. I said they had minutes before they left and if they didn't deal with it now the major was going to have their asses for breakfast tomorrow."

"Gottman."

"Trust me," he replied.

They traveled east, then north up Country Club Estates Drive. It was a barren stretch of land with nothing out there except a few ranches and cattle. They took a hard left on to Las Auras, a dead-end road that cut into the heart of the desert. Already Brody was starting to get a bad feeling about this. He glanced in his mirror at the truck following them.

"I hope you know what you're doing."

"Turn your lights on."

"Why?"

Gottman reached over and flipped the switch. "Confusion. Distraction. It makes it look official." He pointed to a desolate space at the side of the road near an old barn that looked as if it was one windstorm away from being flattened. "Park there."

Brody pulled in and Gottman jumped out.

"Follow my lead."

Gottman pulled his service weapon and pointed it towards the old derelict barn while keeping behind the opened door. By the time Brody got out, the truck behind them had come to a stop. He heard the sound of boots pounding the earth before one of them came up alongside him.

"You got a bead on them?"

"Gottman. You see anything?" Brody shouted, trying to play along. On his side another soldier had taken up position. The two soldiers began talking about the best way to approach it. Gottman gave a nod to Brody and then struck one soldier across his face with the butt of his gun.

The other soldier reacted but it was too late, Brody was on him and took him to the ground. They wrestled on the ground for control and the soldier's gun went off twice. Before he could even attempt to get Brody off him, Gottman came around and knocked him out with his buddy's rifle.

Out of breath, Brody went to get up.

"Right. Strip 'em," Gottman said.

Chapter 11

The evening's conference call between Colonel Lynch, Daniel Sorenson, the president and FEMA representative Margaret Wells had been weighing heavily on Lynch's mind all day. The president wanted to be kept updated on the situation and since the initial outbreak she hadn't spoken with him. It was not just the nation's security that was on the line, it was her career, and she hadn't come this far to lose it now.

On her laptop in front of her the screen was split into four, Daniel Sorenson was beside her looking like a bag of nerves. It would be the first time he'd ever addressed the president and he'd made it clear that he wasn't pleased that it was under these circumstances.

Lynch rubbed her eyes and took a sip of coffee.

The president was the last to join them. She felt her heartbeat speed up as she attempted to put on a brave front, and convey a sense that she had the situation in hand.

"It's under control right now," Lynch said. "As it stands we have it isolated to the hospital here in Alpine and a high school in Marfa. We have been testing those showing symptoms, looking for a possible way of reversing it. Anyone showing symptoms has been isolated and should die within seventy-two hours."

"Those are the known ones, yes?" Wells asked.

Lynch nodded.

"Known ones?" the president asked.

Wells added, "Well it's possible that this has spread beyond the quarantine sites."

Lynch could tell where she was going with this. The contagion may have managed to go beyond that, being as many people visiting the hospital and the school prior to their arrival may have become infected. She could only deal with what was in front of her right now and as it stood, the soldiers that were in the towns hadn't reported any further incidents to the major.

"Colonel?" The president fished for an answer.

"Of course it's possible. However, we are doing the best we can under the circumstances. We have a limited number of soldiers here and even though both towns are small in size, we cannot account for those who might have come in contact with infected citizens before we arrived. But as it stands Major Brown is monitoring the situation minute to minute."

"What a screw-up," the president said before running a hand over his face. "I'm surprised no one has managed to leak out video to the Internet. If the media or public catch wind of this we are going to have a firestorm on our hands that will make Watergate look like child's play."

"Have there been any casualties?" asked Wells.

Lynch dropped her head. She'd received word of two incidents so far, one at the school and one in the hospital, where her men had no other choice but to kill.

"Colonel. Please tell me you have not opened fire," the president said.

As much as she didn't want to insult the man, she wasn't going to stand by and let someone turn the tables on her when he had specifically been the one to guide their actions. "Sir, you instructed us to take whatever measures possible in order to ensure that this did not spread. We are the ones here with boots on the ground trying to handle a matter so this doesn't blow up and affect your position in the next election. We are the ones making the hard decisions. Anyone who has been killed so far would have died within seventy-two hours anyway. The protection of our soldiers and those not infected is the priority here and as you made very clear, we are to ensure this doesn't spread at all costs. Yes. There have been two people killed but both were a threat."

He shook his head, unable to believe that this was happening under his watch. She didn't envy his position. If it ever got out, it wouldn't be her name dragged through the mud, it would be those in the White House. The public would always see people like her as pawns in a game. People trying to serve their country and follow the requests of a leader.

Instead of replying to that, he asked, "What can you

tell me about this? I've read over the report but it doesn't make sense. I feel like there is some information that is being left out."

"You and me both," Sorenson chimed in.

They all directed their gaze to him.

"And you are again?" the president asked.

Sorenson cleared his throat. "Daniel Sorenson, sir. Epidemiologist for the CDC. I'm the one running the tests."

"Ah, well maybe you can shed some light on this mystery."

"I can only tell you what we have discovered so far. It's not much, and some of it is theory right now until we run some more tests."

"Sorenson, just tell me what you know."

He nodded. "If the report reads correctly, the military's goal in Project Icarus was to work with a third-party biotechnology lab to develop advanced forms of bioelectronic medicines that could suppress fear in soldiers so that the chances of success on missions would be higher. Essentially it would deal with fear and anxiety by targeting a specific region of the brain called the amygdala. In a nutshell, this area processes fear, triggers anger, and motivates us to act. Essentially it alerts us to danger and activates our fight-or-flight response. Our basic survival instinct. The prefrontal cortex in which the amygdala resides has been known to control reasoning, judgment and generally helps us to think logically before we act."

"Speak to me in English, Sorenson," the President said in frustration.

Sorenson looked at Lynch and she gave a nod.

"Sir, it's a bit like watching a horror movie. If it's scary and you hear a noise outside, your amygdala might tell you to get up and lock the door. While the prefrontal cortex knows there is no ax murderer outside, you are likely to take action and get up and lock that door. Or let's say you watch a sad movie. Even though someone might not die in the film, you may begin to cry anyway. Essentially certain circumstances can set off false alarms, which unleashes the same level of feeling as if the event was really happening. In a nutshell, it means the brain can't tell what is dangerous and what isn't. Everything seems like a threat. If we take this to the next level, the prefrontal cortex might remember what your nasty ex-partner looked like after she dumped you for someone else. The amygdala is responsible for the surge of fury that you might experience when you see someone that looks even vaguely like your former partner. And 'vaguely' is the specific word here. The amygdala judges whether or not the situation is hazardous. It compares the situation with your past emotionally charged memories. If any of the elements are somewhat similar — the sound of a voice, an expression on a face — the amygdala will set off alarm bells and you will feel an explosion of emotional response."

The president sipped at a glass of water. "Okay but then why are people dying? And why are people harming themselves? Or lashing out?"

Sorenson glanced at the colonel as if making sure it

was okay to share his findings. Lynch made a gesture. "Go ahead, Sorenson, explain what you know," she said.

"Urbach Wiethe disease is a rare genetic disorder that affects individuals neurologically and dermatologically. It is also responsible for damage to the amygdaloid region. If you recall in the report, the studies into creating a drug that could reduce anxiety and fear in our soldiers came to the attention of the military after media outlets began reporting about a subject that couldn't feel fear. The person was suffering from Urbach Wiethe. Based on that information and the studies that were performed, they learned that patient zero showed signs of curiosity towards things that others would usually fear, such as handling live snakes and spiders, and other scenarios that logically most would avoid. Instead of an avoidance reaction, patient zero evoked curiosity. Even in the face of death there was no desperation or urgency."

"This patient had no emotion?"

"No. The patient still had basic emotions such as happiness, sadness, surprise, disgust and anger, but the evolutionary aspect, that survival instinct inside of us that has led us to avoid danger and discomfort, was gone. Instead of processing danger, the patient would go towards it. You name it. Heights, bugs, confined spaces, water, public speaking, needles, even stepping out in front of traffic. We usually will form a negative association with such things, but patient zero was unafraid and curious approaching the very thing that should be avoided. In fact there was a study done on mice that found when the amygdala was damaged, the mice would actually go towards cats. It essentially proved that fearful memories could be erased. This is why the military was excited to study this and incorporate it into their soldiers except it went wrong and they became unstable and it accelerated, so instead of only affecting the amygdala it spread to other parts of the brain and eventually caused death."

"Okay, well that explains the fearless aspect of all of this and the deaths but why are some lashing out?"

"Perception of fear-based threats. They lose all reasoning."

"But you said they exhibit signs of no fear? Which is it?"

"Both, sir. The goal was no fear in the soldiers but it went wrong. This is unstable. Again it's a complex issue, Mr. President. I'm still running tests but what I can determine, based on what has been shared with me and the findings we have learned about since arriving here, is that each patient is essentially experiencing a *pendulum* of emotion. From being fearless and curious, to outright frozen in fear, through to angry and fearful. The best way to understand it is to go back to the hunter-gatherer times. Our basic survival instinct of fight-or-flight was governed by the amygdala. It had to quickly respond to any potential threats. Was something bad? Could it hurt us? It would send a signal to the brain, which in turn would create a response in the body from a flood of adrenaline to react or freeze up the muscles. All of this would happen within a matter of milliseconds so that a person might explode with rage or freeze in fear. It's what we refer to as reacting first, and thinking later. When the amygdala is damaged, instead of being only fearless, we are seeing a range of emotions. People are unstable and eventually adrenaline causes a cardiac arrest. Essentially, Mr. President, these people are losing control, they are at the mercy of their own basic survival instinct."

"Well how have you been able to identify those who have it?"

"Symptoms associated with Urbach Wiethe disease are quite clear but there are also things like headaches, aches, chills, fever, coughing and red eyes. So obviously it's hard to distinguish visually who has it until at least twelve hours into infection. Most would simply consider it as nothing more than flu symptoms, anger and fear."

"And it's transferrable?"

"By way of blood and saliva. Someone coughs on some money and that gets spread around, you now have another infected person. It can be as simple as that. Again though, we are still in the early stages of verifying all of this but over the coming days we should have a more concrete answer for you. Right now we are in foreign territory with this."

He nodded and silence stretched before them all.

"Okay, we need to talk about the worst-case scenario here. First off, what steps are being taken to treat those who have the symptoms? Can it be cured?"

Sorenson chimed in. "We are running trials of different types of drugs on those exhibiting symptoms. So far we haven't seen a change but again there is no cure for Urbach Wiethe disease which was the foundation upon which the initial round of drugs for the soldiers was based."

"We are in contact with the third-party company that was involved in creating it to determine what was used beyond Urbach Wiethe disease samples. We should have an update within the next twenty-four hours," Wells added.

"Make it twelve," the president said in frustration. "This has gone on longer than it should. If for any reason this has breached the towns we may have a national emergency on our hands and if anyone has this and has boarded an international flight this may have gone global. Have there been any reports beyond these two towns?"

"No, sir."

"Well let's hope not."

Lynch saw an opportunity to chime in and provide a glimmer of hope, while at the same time making herself look good and right now she was willing to do whatever it took. "Sir, if I may…" she trailed off.

"Go ahead, colonel."

"We have isolated six people who were exposed to those infected but appear to be immune," she said looking at Sorenson for his support. She raised an eyebrow and Sorenson backed her up.

"That's correct. That's what we are currently working with right now. If we can establish why it's not affecting them or hasn't so far then we might be able to create a cure for this."

"And in the meantime?" the president asked.

"We will take whatever steps are necessary to keep this contained to Alpine and Marfa. However, we may need more troops. Our biggest concern right now is tourists or family members visiting from out of town. They will want to know what is happening so we have to come up with some cover story."

"A gas leak," Wells said.

The president shook his head. "That might work however you won't be able to prevent people from returning back and putting that out to the media. That alone might cause the media to come sniffing for a story. We cannot allow eyes on this scene so this has to be handled immediately."

"And by that you mean?" Sorenson asked, curious. Lynch already knew.

The president didn't reply to that, he said he had another meeting to attend but expected this to be handled as efficiently and as quickly as possible. They had his full support and authorization to take drastic measures to keep it contained. With that, he signed off leaving only the three of them on screen.

Wells dropped her head and sighed. "Colonel Lynch, I

will make arrangements to have a team from FEMA arrive later this evening to offer additional support. If you need more troops I would contact Major Brown and put that into place now. You know what will happen if this situation escapes your hand."

Lynch nodded. She hated being spoken to like a child especially by someone who spent their time reading reports and keeping the president updated. She had no field experience; she didn't understand how delicate the situation was.

But Lynch did.

At the close of the conference call, Sorenson returned to his duties and Lynch got in contact with Major Brown to get an update on the situation over in Marfa and throughout the town of Alpine. She pulled out of her pocket a small bottle of bourbon. She just needed a little something to take the edge off. A quick swig and she picked up the phone.

"What's our current situation, major?"

"Not good."

Her heart leapt into her throat.

"Explain."

"I'm afraid there has been an increase of attacks in the city. Several of our soldiers have gone missing, and we are finding bodies all over the town. We need more soldiers as this is getting out of hand."

"Then you know what to do," she replied.

Chapter 12

They had officially stepped over the line into dangerous, uncharted territory, of that he was sure. Wearing military gear, with their faces covered by masks, they left behind the two soldiers tied up in the back of his truck. Brody had torn out the radio in the unlikely chance the guys managed to escape. It would buy them some time. They had no need to hide the vehicle, as it was pitch dark, that stretch of road had no houses on it and hopefully by the time morning came they would be long gone.

Despite his differences with Jenna, he knew deep down she still loved him but just didn't know how to work through it after all they'd been through, and the hurtful comments they'd made to each other. He'd been unable to recognize her pain because he'd focused only on why he wasn't being heard, and why she wasn't seeing his side of the coin. When reality was, she couldn't. She was lost in her own storm. Then of course there was the time apart that had eaten away at the closeness and bond they once shared, and now they were bordering on estrangement, one of his greatest fears.

"Are you sure you want to do this?" Gottman asked.

"You're asking me that now?" he muttered from behind his mask as they drove the military vehicle towards the medical center.

"Well, better late than never, right?"

"Are you having second thoughts?" Brody asked.

Gottman didn't reply which meant he was at least thinking about it.

"Look, you don't need to go in with me, Gottman. I appreciate what you've done so far but we both don't need to go down for this."

"Chief, as much as I want to say I'm doing this for you, I'm not."

"What?"

"My father is in the hospital. He was taken in a few days ago for surgery related to colon cancer. They are hopeful they can get rid of it but that's still to be seen."

"When did he have the surgery?"

"About a week ago. He was meant to come out this weekend but then all this blew up."

There was a long moment of silence.

"I'm sorry to hear that."

"Ah, he's a strong guy."

"But you don't know if he pulled through?"

"No, I saw him a few days ago and they had him on all these drugs because he's old, and well, he didn't do too well in surgery, but they thought he would recover with time."

Again silence stretched between them. Brody was aware that attempting to get his wife out of there would be challenging but a second person? And one that might not be able-bodied?

"Gottman."

"I know what you're going to say," he replied casting him a sideways glance. "I'm not intending to leave with him."

"You just want to see him?"

He nodded. "And I'm going to stay there."

"What?" he said with an expression of shock hidden behind his mask. "They find out you aren't with the military, you know what will happen."

"I'm not going to leave this gear on, Brody. I'll remove it once we get inside and they'll just think I'm one of the people who are being isolated."

"Yeah, and what happens if you get infected? Huh? Is it really worth losing your life over it? You think that's what your father would want?"

The truck rumbled and they bounced in their seats a little as it hit a couple of potholes. Gottman didn't say anything, instead he reached into his pocket and pulled out a pack of smokes and pulled off his mask.

"What are you doing?"

"Having one last smoke. This shit has got my nerves on edge."

Brody chuckled. Besides a few military jeeps that zipped by, the town seemed desolate at least on the stretch of road they were traveling. As they drove around the loop and along Hendryx Avenue, Brody spotted lights in the distance. Several military vehicles were blocking the road.

"Gottman, put your mask back on."

He eased off the gas, and Gottman tossed the cigarette out the window.

There had to have been at least six soldiers patrolling and monitoring the road. He brought the window down as they got closer. The smell of diesel from the truck lingered making Brody feel even more queasy. Brody glanced down at the badge above his breast pocket, it had the last name Patrick on it.

"Your name," Brody said as they rolled closer to the checkpoint. The blockade was new as it wasn't there on the way back. Things must have been getting worse in town.

"What?"

"Your name, remember it."

Gottman glanced down, his badge had the name

Diego. "Shit. Just my luck. I don't look like a Diego. Let's hope they don't ask us to take off our masks." Two soldiers stepped in front of the truck; one of them had a hand raised. Brody applied the brakes, which squealed ever so slightly. The soldiers parted going around either side.

"Where you heading?"

"To the medical center. Any update?" Brody asked trying to act all nonchalant.

The soldier looked back at the checkpoint. "Yeah, things are getting wild. We've had to drop a few locals. I hope they are getting reinforcements as I'm not sure how long we are going to hold back the tide."

"Damn. That bad?"

He nodded looking back at him and shining a flashlight at his mask.

"Taking precautions?"

"Can't be too careful," Brody said. The soldier nodded and then raised his hand to the checkpoint to let them through.

"All right, you're free to go."

Inwardly Brody breathed a sigh of relief. But just as they were about to pull away, another soldier jogged up shining a flashlight up at the vehicle. "Hey Diego, I've been meaning to have a word with you."

Shit, Brody thought as the soldier blocked the way forward. He had to think fast. Seconds. That's all they had as he made his way around and banged on the side of the truck, wanting him to bring the window down. Then it came to him.

"That's probably not a good idea. You might want to tell him to back up."

"Why?" the soldier asked while adjusting his grip on the rifle. A shot of cold fear went through Brody.

"He's been exposed. That's why I'm taking him to the hospital."

"What?" The soldier on Brody's side yelled to the other guy to back up.

Both soldiers took a few steps back.

"Are you exposed?"

"No but that's why I'm wearing this gear. Look, I need to get him to the hospital. Just to make sure."

"Right." He jerked his rifle towards the now open checkpoint. "Go on through. I hope he makes it."

"Me too."

Brody gave the truck some gas and rolled forward. All the way, sweat dripped down the side of his face.

"Nice move," Gottman said peering at the side mirror to see if they were following. They weren't. The checkpoint closed up and they continued on their way north. When they made it into the parking lot, Brody killed the engine and they hopped out. "For a while there I was wondering how we were going to get through but I guess we have the story to get us inside," Gottman added.

"That was for back there. If we say that now they are going to isolate you probably alongside other infected people. No. We can't do that."

"Then I hope you have a good idea for getting in the door."

"I thought you did?" Brody asked.

Gottman shrugged. "I got us the clothes. I don't work miracles."

They trudged towards the building, this time taking one of the side exits to avoid running into the same soldier they'd spoken to earlier. Around the building soldiers had been posted by all the exits. Brody could feel beads of sweat forming on his brow as they approached two of them.

"Hey there, we've been asked to relieve you. They want you down at the checkpoint on Hendryx Avenue."

"Hendryx Avenue? How come we didn't hear about this?"

"Look, it's your call. If you want to deal with disciplinary action from the major, be my guest but he was chewing out some poor kid back at the checkpoint for disobeying a direct order. I felt sorry for the guy. His radio wasn't working so it wasn't his fault but the major didn't see it that way. Fucking guy's a lunatic." Brody shook his head and scanned the perimeter before fixing his gaze on the guy in front of him.

The soldier looked at his buddy and then nodded. They took over their position and once they were out of sight, Brody pulled the doors open and stepped in.

"I'm starting to understand why they chose you over me," Gottman said, chuckling behind his mask.

* * *

Jenna had been isolated with a group of five other staff members — a security guard, another nurse, a lab technician, someone from the pharmacy and an orderly. The room had no windows and no clock on the wall, and they had been relieved of cell phones, watches, and stripped of clothes and were now wearing hospital gowns and paper-thin blue foot covers. She was uncomfortable, overheated and her patience was wearing thin. She wasn't the only one that thought the same. For the past two hours they'd taken turns venting.

"They're treating us like lab rats," the orderly said banging on the door with his fist.

"Stop doing that," the tech said. "You'll only incite them."

"Ah, who cares?" He banged again.

"I care. It's starting to piss me off."

The orderly raised both hands and pulled a face. "Well, I'm sorry, did I ruin your peace?"

The tech guy got up to confront him but Jenna was quick to get between them. "Let's not do this. Let it go. I think we've all had our buttons pushed and we're tired and hungry."

He scowled and nodded. "Yeah, I'm hungry."

"What's your name?" Jenna asked the orderly.

"Michael."

"How long have you been working here?"

"Six months."

"You from Alpine?"

"What is this? Twenty questions?"

The tech got up again and Jenna only had to flash him the hand and he backed off.

"Listen, we're in here together. So we might as well get along."

Michael shrugged then said, "A year. I've been in

Alpine a year. Now I wish I had never moved here."

"What brought you here?"

"A girl. Thought she was my soul mate. Crazy, huh?"

Jenna thought of Brody for a second.

Michael continued. "We met on vacation. I used to live in New York but she convinced me to move out here. A dumb choice. That's for sure."

"What went wrong?"

"She had issues. Deep issues. Mental issues. I told her to get help but she refused. I mean she did get some help initially but she just kept blaming me for every little thing. What started out as good slowly got worse until we couldn't stand being around each other. Anyway, she moved out and that was it."

"So you feel better for it?"

"No. I miss her like crazy. But what can I do?"

Jenna nodded and thought back to her last conversation with Brody before she packed her bags and walked out the door heading for her parents' home. The pain of losing Will had taken its toll. It had formed a wedge between them. While she wanted to talk about it, see counselors and work through it, Brody had acted as though it wasn't affecting him, but it was. His lack of desire to talk about it led to them rarely talking. He would come home from work, eat dinner, watch TV and go to bed and do it all over again. The spark in their marriage dimmed until she was unable to meet his needs. Physical contact which had never been a thing before soon became an issue. She just wanted her space to heal while he desperately wanted to connect. She couldn't give him that. At least not while she was still reeling from losing Will. But it wasn't just that. At least that's what her therapist had said. There was more behind it. Deep-rooted issues from her childhood that had found their way to the surface and in the hardest moments of her pain only made her push him away. Eventually they just got to a point where it was uncomfortable to be around each other. She didn't know when the next disagreement would turn into blaming or if he would lose his temper and leave. Soon fear took hold and everything made her afraid. Being alone, being with him, thinking of the future. It wasn't healthy for him or her so she left hoping that space might bring them together. It hadn't. They became estranged and in time she felt the only option that remained was to let him go. It was unfair to hold him captive and not allow him to get on with his life, or find someone who didn't have all the hangups she did. The whole thing had broken her heart.

"… Anyway, that's old news. Here we are stuck in shitville dealing with this crap," Michael said. "They do not pay me enough for this. The first thing I'm going to do when I get out of here is quit."

"Geesh, I wish you would quit. Quit bitching," the tech said.

Michael scowled at him and took a few steps forward.

Before another argument between them could begin, the sound of gunfire erupted. It was a steady staccato, loud but partially dulled by the thick door that separated them from the hallway in the lower level of the hospital.

Chapter 13

Jenna joined Michael at the door as they pressed their ears against it to try and figure out what was going on. There was a lot of shouting, several people screaming, soldiers giving direct orders for someone to back up, then more gunfire. Soon, what sounded like only the military attempting to control a violent confrontation turned into total chaos. Yelling, shouting, doors banging, glass breaking, guns firing and gurneys being slammed into the walls.

They took a step back as something hard collided with the door.

What sounded like a person being thrown against the door turned into multiple thuds like someone kicking the door.

More gunfire, and it stopped.

The sound of a key in the lock, and the door swung open. There was a soldier waving them out. "We've had a breach, follow me."

Outside two more soldiers were on either side of the doorway, rifles raised. Before Jenna had taken a step towards the exit, one of them unleashed a deafening flurry of rounds. "Matthews, there's too many of them. We need to take a different route."

All six of them streamed out into the chaotic scene. A bloody handprint was smeared on the wall, a gurney was turned on its side, paperwork was lying all over the floor like confetti and there were brass shell cases surrounding multiple victims, some dead, others bleeding out. Jenna's eyes widened, her jaw dropped.

"Ma'am, move it!" the soldier said giving her a push towards the south wing. She was followed by Michael and the other four as the sound of gunfire echoed loudly. It was the closest thing to what she imagined war was like in the Middle East. An endless stream of shouting, shooting and devastation. The walls were peppered with rounds, and slumped over a desk was Dr. David Summers. His arms hung down, blood dripping off the hands. She wanted to scream but no words escaped her mouth. It felt like she was moving in slow motion as she was thrust forward.

"Move it."

The staccato of gunfire was so overwhelming that she'd frozen in the middle of the hallway, staring at Summers. That's when she felt someone grab her by the wrist and pull her forward. It was Michael. "Come on."

Out the corner of her eye she watched as four patients rushed forward straight into the line of fire. Like dominoes they dropped under a hail of bullets. Led into a stairwell, they began making the ascent with two soldiers at the front and another in the rear.

"Where are we going?" Michael bellowed but the soldiers were too focused on plowing through anyone that came at them and it seemed as if the whole damn hospital had gone nuts. The halls were in complete disarray on the main level, a window at the far end of the corridor had been smashed, and several bodies lay on the ground.

Then she saw a woman and some men hunched over

what appeared to be a soldier. They were driving a steel rod repeatedly into him. He must have been dead, as his body wasn't moving but that didn't stop them from obsessively striking him. While those they saw were infected, as their skin looked leathery and their eyes bloodshot, there were others who appeared to be just caught up in it. Prevented from leaving by soldiers, they were either shot or taken down by the infected. Fear gripped Jenna as they hurried down a hallway only to come face to face with a large knot of people that were going berserk. The soldiers opened fire, and Jenna saw a kid who couldn't have been more than ten years of age drop.

"Stop!"

But her words were wasted. No one was listening. It was a matter of survival and they weren't taking any chances. Forced through a door, Jenna stumbled and her knee slammed into the hard floor. She let out a cry, but was promptly hauled to her feet by the soldier behind her while the other two provided cover. She couldn't understand how this had got out of control so fast. Where had all these people come from? There were a fair number in the medical center but nowhere close to the amount she'd seen down the hallway. Dashing down one more corridor they were led into a room where the doctor she'd seen earlier that day was under the watchful protection of two more soldiers.

"Any more, sir?" one of the three escorting soldiers asked.

"There are another six in the west wing."

"That's overrun."

"We need them."

The soldier nodded and they left them behind with the doctor and the two soldiers. As soon as the door was closed behind them, one of the two soldiers watching over the doc stepped forward and locked the door before removing his mask.

Jenna frowned in disbelief. "Brody?"

He hurried over to her and grabbed her firmly by her shoulders. "You okay?"

"Yeah. But what's going on?"

He looked over to the doc, at which point the other soldier removed his mask. "Hi Jenna," Gottman said, an expression of sadness on his face. Gottman had found his father in the hospital but he was no longer the same man. He'd succumb to the pandemic that had befallen many. He had no other choice than to leave him behind.

"There's no time to explain. We need to get out of here. The doc here is going to help, aren't you, doc?" Gottman said sticking a rifle into his side. He winced and reached around to the back of his head, and brought out a hand covered in blood.

"What did you do?" she asked.

"Ah it's just a flesh wound," Gottman said. "Made him a little more compliant, didn't it, doc?" Gottman put his mask back on and the doc led them to the rear of the room, through another door into an adjoining room and then into a hall that was empty. It was mostly used for technicians taking blood samples between different labs and it wasn't exposed to the main arteries that ran through the hospital. Having worked there for long enough Jenna knew he was leading them to an exit on the east side. As the doctor moved down the hall, he used his card to buzz through doors into restricted areas. All the while the steady echo of gunfire kept them all in a state of uneasiness.

"We have a truck on the east side that will get us away from here," Brody said.

Jenna looked him up and down as they moved through the corridors. "Why?"

"What?" he asked keeping a steady pace behind the doctor.

"Why did you come here?"

"Well it wasn't for a checkup," he said with a smile. Her lip curled then her half-smile disappeared. There wasn't time to get into it though she was curious to know why he would risk his career, and life to get her out. It wasn't like she had given him reason. If anything she had made it clear that she no longer wanted contact. And in all honesty, she wasn't sure he really cared. Her thoughts shifted to the divorce papers. Had he signed them? She shook her head. It didn't matter. Right now getting the hell out of there was priority number one.

"Go, go, go!" Brody said waving on the small group as he moved to the back of the line in preparation of accessing the next corridor, which would take them back into the guts of the hospital. From there it was a clear shot to the exit, approximately a hundred yards. The door beeped as Sorenson swiped his card over the reader. Gottman pulled it open and was immediately confronted by a knife-wielding woman who was drenched from head to toe in blood. Instead of shooting her, he reared back his rifle and slammed the butt into her face knocking her out cold.

There was no time to gawk.

They stepped over her and pressed on, moving quickly while scanning the left and right for additional threats. Ten yards and a heavyset guy holding a shotgun walked around the corner and before Gottman could react, he unloaded a round knocking Janice, the other nurse, back into the wall. Her only saving grace was that she died quickly. Gottman returned fire and a round struck the guy in the shoulder causing him to drop the shotgun, but the situation only got worse as three severely infected patients barreled around the corner.

"Brody!"

He couldn't help as he was also fighting off a patient who'd picked up a dead soldier's rifle. The damn thing still had half of his arm attached to it.

"Get into one of the rooms," Brody shouted to the others who were sandwiched between the onslaught. Jenna darted through the nearest door, while a couple of the others went into another. What seemed like a good idea, turned out to be a mistake.

She turned just in time to see a man wield a shiny object.

It struck her in the face, knocking her unconscious.

Chapter 14

The magnitude of the situation bore down as they arrived on the outskirts of Marfa High School. Something had gone terribly wrong. Along the way they'd seen vehicles on fire in the middle of the road with engines still running, doors open and the drivers missing, as if they'd abandoned them in a hurry. There was a six-car pileup on Murphy Street, and a riot between soldiers south of Mesa Street so they had to head east on Washington. Nick glanced at a white truck as they passed by. Its windshield was smashed in. There was blood on the hood and a woman lying motionless on the ground. Her skull caved in. To the left, a large truck had taken out a wall, collided into a home and set it on fire but the fire service wasn't out trying to extinguish the flames. Under the cover of night they saw the silhouettes of people running, and heard the echo of gunfire. Two darted in front of their vehicle and Emerick had to slam on the brakes causing them to jolt forward in their seats. It was as if the whole damn town had decided to turn on each other. By the time they had the school in sight he could tell things were not the same. The doors were wide open, the military trucks gone and there were multiple dead soldiers. Emerick eased off the gas and looked out trying to make sense of it.

"What the hell has happened?" Angela said.

Nick went to get out and Emerick cautioned him. "Wait! Let me go in first. Stay here."

"If you're going in, so am I. You'll need someone to watch your back."

He nodded and hopped out. Emerick went around to the back of the truck and pulled out the rifle, and tucked the Glock into the small of his back. "Stay close."

"Don't I get a handgun?" Nick asked.

He scowled. "Kid, not even if you were the last person on the planet."

Emerick told Angela to keep the doors locked, and if they saw soldiers approach, to drive away. They would meet them back at the baseball diamond. She nodded and the last thing Nick heard was the sound of the doors locking.

With that said they ran at a crouch towards the school. Nick glanced back at Angela and Callie and tried to give a reassuring smile but it probably just came across as nervous. It was so quiet. A far cry from the sounds of gunfire and soldiers talking among themselves when they left. They entered a set of double doors at the rear of the school, and stepped over some dead soldiers. All of their weapons had been taken. Whoever had engaged with them had made sure to take what they wanted.

"You think the parents did this?"

"It's possible," Emerick said peering into the dark hallway. Their boots echoed slightly as they moved inside. Nick glanced over his shoulder to check behind him. The fear of encountering someone like Emerick's neighbor stuck in his mind. He couldn't shake the image of the blood running down his chest, and the knife in his hand, or seeing the shock on Emerick's face after he killed him.

If police were now looking for his killer, they had to be far away as they hadn't heard a single siren since heading for the school.

"Where did they put them?"

"In the gymnasium."

Nick was certain that any second now a soldier was going to appear and they'd both find themselves zip tied and joining the others, but that idea soon left his mind as they rounded the corner that led to the gym. The doors, which were once sealed, were wide open and it was clear that the students were gone, but the question was where?

It smelled like urine and puke inside the gym.

Nick used the flashlight on his phone to illuminate the way. The light washed over a few faces he recognized. Debbie Gunther. A bullet had penetrated her skull. Keith Carson's back was riddled with wounds. Nick lifted his top to cover the lower half of his mouth. He wasn't sure this was related to a pandemic but he wasn't taking any chances. Who knew what was driving people insane? Was it airborne?

Emerick stopped and pulled his phone out. "You check over there. We're not leaving until I make sure my boy isn't here." They parted and Emerick searched the east side of the gym while Nick dealt with the opposite end. He stepped over multiple bodies and his stomach twisted. Why would the military open fire on a bunch of students? Not all of them were there, leading him to believe the vast majority had been led away, but sixteen were lying inside that room. It looked as if they had fanned out and attempted to escape. The windows above the bleachers were shattered. The walls were peppered with rounds, and blood was everywhere. It was like being in a nightmare that he couldn't wake up from.

"You found anything?" Emerick asked.

"No. You?"

He shook his head, staring down at lifeless corpses. "Nothing."

Just as they were making their way out of there, Nick swore he heard something but couldn't place it. "Emerick. Did you hear that?"

"What?"

They stood still.

Emerick waved him off. "Forget it. It's probably just your imagination."

They took a few more steps and then both of them heard it. It was a groan coming from their right, over by the climbing ropes. Nick hurried over to find Nancy Ritalin alive. She was barely hanging on to life. She had two wounds — one to her shoulder and the other to her left leg. Based on the amount of blood it was clear she had lost a considerable amount, and should have already been dead.

"Nick, stay back," Emerick bellowed.

Nick shook his head and dropped down to a knee. "Nancy. What happened?"

Her eyes focused in and she recognized him. "Nick?"

They didn't really know each other nor did they hang out in the same circle of friends but she was one of those people that always would say hello, and had a smile on her face. Just a good person.

"Nancy. Where are the others?"

She coughed. "They took them out of here on the school buses. I don't know where." She gasped and heaved again as if speaking was too difficult. Her eyes closed and Nick had to shake her to keep her conscious.

"Nancy, why did the military open fire?"

"They didn't. There were others that made their way in, sick people, like Toby Winters. They had guns and just..." She took a deep breath and then just like that she was gone.

"Nancy. Nancy!" Nick yelled.

"She's gone, Nick. We need to leave."

He couldn't believe this was happening. It seemed surreal, like he was walking in a dream state unable to escape. Emerick grabbed him by the collar and hoisted him to his feet, pulling him towards the door. Nick kept looking at her until they disappeared around the corner.

"They couldn't have gone far. Not under these conditions."

"There were a lot of soldiers," Nick said.

"Maybe. But there are a lot of residents. I wouldn't have been the only concerned parent that showed up here. Uncle Sam made a big mistake, thinking they could come into our neck of the woods and do whatever the hell they liked."

Moving down the corridor they made it to the back doors and pushed out to find the Chevy gone. "What the heck?"

"Maybe they encountered hostiles," Nick said.

The sound of yelling could be heard nearby.

They strode towards the road and came around the corner to find about twenty people attacking one another. Three individuals spotted Nick and began running towards them.

"Fall back," Emerick said to Nick, pushing him with one arm while raising the rifle with the other. He unloaded two rounds, taking out the one closest to them before he turned and they dashed back into the school, slamming the door behind them. Frantically Nick looked for anything to hold the doors in place but there was nothing, then he looked down at a dead soldier. He crouched and undid his belt, pulling it out as he rolled him over. Then he wound the thick leather around the door handles and tightened it.

No sooner had he done that than he felt the door being pulled from the other side. They stumbled back and dashed into the heart of the school. Trapped. Isolated. And surrounded by threats.

* * *

Forty minutes earlier, Sergio and Lars had returned to Alpine with one goal in mind — finding the coroner's office and disposing of Viola's body. He had all but made up his mind that he was ready to kill if need be to avoid jail time. Sergio had berated himself on the drive back while Lars remained silent. It was for the best as he'd considered shooting him and leaving his body out in the desert too. Having one other person know about Viola death was one too many. What if the cops brought in Lars? What if they wore him down? It wouldn't be the first time someone close had turned in a friend, or family member to get a reduced sentence. The only reason he was keeping him alive was he needed his assistance. He couldn't do this alone.

That all changed when they arrived back in Alpine and headed for the hospital.

The dirt bikes idled at the edge of the road as Sergio looked at the roadblock up ahead. "What is going on?"

"Dear God, do you not listen? I told you about this," Lars said. "They've been here all day."

He jerked his head towards another road, and pulled away expecting Lars to follow. Sergio glanced in his mirror to check. As much as Lars might have wanted to fly the coop, he was in this as much as Sergio. He might not have been the one to wrap his hands around Viola's throat but he dug the grave. Sergio made sure of that. If he was going down he wasn't going alone.

Sergio jerked forward, dizzy on gasoline fumes. His adrenaline had kicked in as he felt the dirt bike rattle between his legs. A quick squeeze of the clutch and he shifted up a gear. As they soared down the road, his eyes widened as he saw multiple vehicles on fire. Suddenly a guy darted out with a baseball bat. He swung it with violent intention to knock Sergio's head clean off. He ducked and the bike wobbled beneath him. The bat skimmed the top of his motorcycle helmet. A glance in the mirror revealed Lars wasn't as lucky. The guy quickly adjusted and this time punched the bat directly into Lars' stomach. He flew off, and the bike slammed into a car, crumpling, the back wheel still spinning madly as the engine roared. Sergio jerked the handles on his bike, and skidded around, heading back to help him. Lars looked as if he was out cold, as the madman came towards him, gearing up for the finale. He raised his bat just as Sergio reached around, pulled his Glock and squeezed off a round. The attacker's legs buckled and he dropped to his knees as Sergio soared by him firing one more into the back of his head. He brought the bike to a stop, and hopped off near Lars.

"Lars!"

As much as he banged heads with him and had

considered taking him out, it was just hot air, frustration and worry driving him. He had few friends in the world but Lars was his closest. That's why he'd helped him dispose of Viola. He could have turned him down, hell, he could have phoned the police but instead he showed up willing to do whatever. Sergio removed his helmet and gave him a few slaps. "Come on, buddy."

His eyes started blinking, and then he coughed, and that was followed by a large gasp before more coughing occurred. "Holy shit. You had me worried there for a minute."

"What happened?" Lars asked.

"Some maniac just scored a home run."

He frowned and then his memory came back. He was quick to look past Sergio. Behind them was the body of the asshole.

"Is he alive?"

"If he is, he would damn well be a living miracle," Sergio said before laughing and shoving the Glock back into the small of his back. He hauled him to his feet and

Lars put his hands on his knees and took a deep breath. Sergio patted him on the back as Lars tried to get his bearings. He looked over at his bike, which was a complete write-off.

"Shit."

"Ah don't worry, jump on the back of mine."

They turned to head towards it when bullets ricocheted off the tops of nearby cars. Both of them hit the ground trying to get a bead on the shooter. "Where's that coming from?"

"I don't know. I can't see a damn thing out here."

The streets were dark, even the street lamps had been turned off which was unusual. Both of them scrambled to the closest car to take cover. Sergio pulled out his Glock and prepared to return fire but the shooting had stopped. He didn't like sitting where they were, who knew if the shooter was changing position.

"We need to move."

Lars agreed and they scrambled over to the next car, staying low. The very second they came out from the vehicle more gunfire erupted, this time a bullet struck Lars in the leg. He let out a loud cry and buckled. Sergio grasped and dragged him out of the gap between the vehicles.

"I've been hit," he said, grasping his upper leg.

Sergio looked at it and shook his head before trying to peer through the car window to get a better idea of where their attackers were. Whoever it was they were going to pay for this. "Stay here."

Lars grabbed his arm. "What? Don't leave me here."

"I'm not, you idiot. I need to find this guy otherwise we aren't getting out of here."

First he needed to see where the rounds were coming from. Because it was dark there was a chance he would see the flash from the muzzle but that meant exposing himself and potentially putting himself at risk.

There was no other option.

He darted out, while keeping his face to the east. He was sure that the rounds were coming from the apartment block just down from them but... *Pop. Pop. Pop.* Rounds lanced car windows, sending glass fragments over him. It was close but worth it. He spotted the flash of a muzzle three stories above. *Right you bastard, you are mine!* He instinctively checked the rounds in his gun and then darted out into the night to kill again.

Chapter 15

Gottman killed the lunatic. He hurried in and scanned the room for more threats before reaching down and trying to wake Jenna. She was out cold. Blood trickled down the side of her temple. He could see she was breathing but they'd need to tend to that wound soon. He placed her left arm over his shoulders, and looped his right around her waist and hauled her to her feet. Across the way, in the adjoining room, the lab technician cowered. A look of fear masked his face as he gripped the doorway

"You!" Gottman shouted. "What's your name?"

"Liam."

"Well, Liam, I need you..."

As the words left his mouth another crazed maniac charged into the room. With his rifle hand wrapped around Jenna, he couldn't bring up the rifle fast enough.

Fortunately he didn't need to. Two rounds erupted,

and the asshole dropped.

Running into view was Brody. His eyes darted between them and he rushed in to help. "What the hell happened?"

"She knocked herself out, what do you think?" he said. Again he motioned for Liam to hurry over. Liam darted across the corridor like a scared mouse and took his place so Gottman could check for threats. The other three were out of sight. There was a momentary break in the chaos allowing him to find the others and tell them to grab anything they could use as a weapon. The problem was none of them except Michael had much training in weapons. He scooped up the shotgun that had killed Nancy and they continued on until they reached the exit. A swift kick to the door and it burst open into the parking lot where fires were raging and illuminating the night.

Gottman's jaw dropped when he saw their truck was gone.

* * *

Gottman went into panic mode.

"No. NO. NO!" He scanned his field of vision, searching the lot of cars, many had been destroyed. It was as if they had entered a war zone, and someone had thrown Molotov cocktails at vehicles. The fire crackled as it ate away at the insides of vehicles.

Brody emerged clutching Jenna with Liam on the other side.

"It's gone. It's gone," Gottman said punching the air with his fist and cursing loudly. In policing you had to adapt to changing situations. One minute you could be pulling someone over for a busted taillight, the next, dodging bullets. They worked in a state of discomfort, making split decisions on the fly. This was no different.

"We'll find another vehicle, let's just keep moving." Brody turned to an orderly who had offered to take Jenna.

"The name's Michael," he said.

Brody was hesitant but knew that it would serve them better if he was protecting their six. Several screams cut into the night, close by, enough to scare the shit out of them and make them move. They were going to need a vehicle to make it to Marfa, but right now it was about survival, nothing more. When they entered the building, it was peaceful and calm. How quickly everything had taken a turn for the worse. Sorenson looked in a state of shock. His eyes were wide like a deer caught in headlights. They hurried south trying to put as much distance as possible between them and the hospital which now had smoke rising above it on the north side. However, they didn't make it far. On the south side a strong force of military was still there engaging with a crowd of people who were inside the building but had taken out the windows and were returning fire.

Gottman held a fist up, peering around the corner before directing everyone to go left towards the trees. There was very little to hide behind, it was mostly flat desert plains with few shrubs and trees. If it weren't for the night they would have been spotted.

The sound of gunfire faded as they walked further

southeast. Brody knew the Alpine Area Engineer Maintenance facility was a few miles south, and across from that an RV park. He had to wonder if some of the maniacs came from that park.

The group walked in silence, shock setting in, and questions rising.

Brody glanced at Jenna; her head hung low, toes dragging as the two men carried her. He jogged up to the doctor near the front of the group.

"Sorenson." He turned. "You want to fill in the blanks?"

He shrugged. "It's a pandemic."

"Well no shit. What are we dealing with?"

"Well it isn't zombies," Gottman said, "because when you kill them they don't get back up. That is right, doc?"

He nodded, and scoffed finding humor in Gottman's analysis. "They're just ordinary people. Like anyone who might contract Ebola."

"Except this isn't Ebola, is it?"

He shook his head as they continued trudging south.

They could just make out the lights of RV vans in the distance. Little pinpricks of luminescent amber light. The sound of generators could be heard churning over.

"You work for the military?" Brody asked.

"I was brought in by the military. I work for the CDC out of Chicago."

"Why would they bring you in when they have their own people?"

"For testing."

"Testing for what?" Gottman asked looking over his shoulder to make sure the group was safe.

"It's called the amygdala syndrome."

"The what?" Brody asked.

"The military was working on a new form of drug to enhance soldiers. Initially it was created from studies into dealing with PTSD and memories. At some point they began to look at the fight-or-flight response, our basic survival instinct and the possibilities of removing fear and anxiety."

"Great. Uncle Sam isn't satisfied with getting people to

sign up, now they want lab rats," Brody said.

"It was done with the best intentions."

"Yeah?" Gottman said. "Then how did we end up in this mess?" He adjusted his rifle between his two arms and spat on the ground.

"Look, this isn't new. They were testing all forms of drugs back in the Vietnam War. Back then they were giving them drugs like speed, steroids and painkillers to help them deal with extended combat. They've just ramped things up since then."

"So you're telling me all these maniacs that we've encountered were the end result of what the military was trying to create?"

"No. No, it went wrong."

"No shit," Gottman said without even looking at him. Sorenson glanced at him then back at Brody. He was about to explain more but it would have to wait as they were close to the RV park and needed to have their wits about them. The park had enough sites for up to seventy RVs including big rigs. The structures on site were used for a welcoming area, office, shop, cabins, washrooms, showers, playground and a rec room. It was popular with the tourists in the summer months and this summer was no exception. However, it looked different than it usually did with some of the cabins on fire, and several RVs abandoned, and many having collided with one another as if attempting to make an escape.

Brody turned to the others and told them to wait among the ponderosa pines while he and Gottman checked it out. Surrounding the entire park were pine trees that had been planted to provide privacy, and to give people a sense they were in the woods when in reality they were smack bang in the middle of an arid desert. The group huddled together as Brody and Gottman ran at a crouch towards an RV where the door was wide open. They darted inside and Brody used his cell to provide light. It looked like whoever had been there had left in a hurry as they'd left two plates of food on the counter, and the stove was still on. All that concerned Brody was seeing if the keys were still in the ignition — they weren't. They began rooting around looking for them but didn't have much success so they exited and tried another one.

It was a bad mistake.

Inside a man lay on the floor of the RV, his guts hanging out of his stomach, and the knife that had torn him open embedded in his chest.

"Geesh. Animals," Gottman said stepping over him and making his way down to the front. He checked the ignition. Nothing. Brody checked the glove compartment, and then Gottman pulled down the sun visor and keys jangled as they hit the seat. "Ah, bingo!"

"Let's get him out."

They returned to the rear and Gottman went to lift the dead man and Brody yelled, "No. Put your gloves on. We can't take any chances." He nodded and after slipping into gloves they hauled him out of there.

Just as they dropped his body and were about to reboard, they heard a woman screaming, "No! Come back with my baby."

Brody turned and Gottman grabbed his arm. "Leave it.

We can't help."

He nodded, and took a few steps towards the RV as the screaming persisted. He couldn't just stand by and do nothing. Call it instincts. Duty. Or human decency. He patted Gottman on the back as he was stepping into the RV. "Start it up. I'll be right back."

"Chief."

"Just do it!" he said tearing away and running in the direction of the screams. It was pitch black out. No stars in the sky. Besides the screams from the woman it was eerily quiet for an RV park. He pounded the ground, crossing over into row B, and darting between two RVs before coming out and finding a woman sitting near the rec room on a bench holding a baby in one hand and a handgun in the other. The lady screaming was standing nearby pleading with her to give back her baby. One glance at the woman under the glow of the moon made it clear she was infected. Her skin had turned leathery, her eyes were bloodshot and her nose was running.

While Sorenson hadn't explained how the infection

was transferred, Brody was certain that the odds of that child not becoming infected were slim to none. The woman was pressing her face against the baby and clutching it like it was the most precious thing in her life. She reminded him of some of the drug addicts he'd found in a crack house a few months back — women and men strung out on drugs, their eyes sallow, and cheeks gaunt, and a lifeless dead look to their gaze.

Brody scanned his surroundings for threats before circling around the rec room. He figured if he could get the gun out of her hand that would at least give the baby some chance of survival. He wasn't going to shoot her, at least not with the baby in hand. As he came into view, the woman who was screaming spotted him. He put a finger up to his lips and pulled back behind the corner. He looked around for anything he could wield — something long and sturdy. A quick decision to dart over to an RV, and he returned with a long pole that was attached to the top of the vehicle using bungee cords. It looked like the kind of thing that might have been used to hang washing out. It was close to six feet in length. The woman was still there when he returned.

He studied her movements. They went in an obsessive cycle. She would bring the barrel of the gun up to the child, at which point the mother would cry out and that would cause her to aim it at her. But she hadn't squeezed the trigger. Why? He'd seen the way the others were in the hospital, they didn't hesitate. Was it possible she was still in the early stage of the infection? Was each person affected differently? Was it slowly but surely overtaking them like a crippling disease?

Brody made his move. Slowly he closed the gap between them while her arm was outstretched with the gun. He reared back the metal rod and brought it down hard just behind the wrist, and hit hard enough to break it. The gun dropped, clattering on the ground, and he kicked it away as the mother came rushing in and grabbed her baby. It all happened so quickly.

The woman was lying on the ground screaming in pain as Brody turned to leave.

He'd been so focused on the woman he didn't notice the crowd of people closing in. By the time he spotted them his escape route was gone.

They stared at him, some twitched others sneered.

All of them were suffering from different degrees of the disease.

Brody turned 360 degrees and realized why so many had become infected. All it took was one, and it would spread. "Back off!" Brody yelled, swiping the air with the steel rod and trying to protect the scared mother who was clutching her crying child. The large group lunged and Brody backed into the cabin rec room behind them with the woman and the kid. He closed the door and locked it. But they weren't out of the woods yet, the crowd was moving in on them.

Chapter 16

The sound of glass shattering sent a cold jolt of fear coursing through Nick's body. He and Emerick were searching for an alternative route out of the school but scanning the windows they could see more and more people moving in on the school. Many were fighting each other, as if under threat, while others were rattling locked doors on the school, smashing glass and climbing.

"Kid, you ever fired a gun?"

Nick frowned. "What happened to being the last person on the planet?"

"That was then, this is now." Emerick removed the Glock and in a matter of seconds took him through a few simple steps of loading and unloading a gun, clearing a jam and aiming. It was foundational. Stuff he already knew from his old man. While his father hadn't let him shoot a weapon, he wasn't opposed to letting him hold an unloaded gun. He didn't want him to be afraid of them.

It was all about common sense. Treating every weapon as if it was loaded, never pointing at anything you didn't intend to kill, and understanding that it wasn't a toy. He didn't want to burst Emerick's bubble as he showed him how to grip it. Nick remembered when he fourteen and his father took him out the back of their house and showed him the exact same thing. In that moment his mind drifted to better days, times when his father and mother got on well. And when they weren't fighting, slamming doors, or reversing down the driveway.

"So you got that, kid?"

He nodded.

"Keep that gun pointed in a safe direction, and always keep your finger off that trigger until ready to shoot. You understand. And whatever the fuck you do. Do not point it at me. You got it?"

"Yeah, yeah, I got it."

He slapped him on the back. "Let's move to higher ground."

They dashed down the corridor and slipped into a

stairwell and took two steps at a time until they were on the second floor. As they moved past classrooms, Nick's heart was thumping hard in his chest. His breathing was fast as the ever-present sense of danger heightened. As they wandered down the empty hallway, Emerick was making suggestions on what they should do. Hide in one of the classrooms. Find an open window and climb out onto the roof. Or just wait it out and hope to God that no one came up the second floor. Nick was listening and was about to reply when a dark blur shot out knocking Emerick to the floor. In the dark it was hard to see. All Nick could determine was that it had Emerick by the throat and was attempting to kill him. They wrestled around on the floor until they rolled into a shard of light filtering in from the moon. That's when Nick saw it was a soldier, the same one he'd seen outside before they had made their escape. He had short blond hair, a granite jaw, and was outfitted in the same military gear, minus the helmet. While his skin looked the same, there was clearly something unstable about him.

"Shoot him!" Emerick said trying his best to get the muscular soldier off him. It was near impossible. This was a man who was trained to kill. Emerick's rifle had dropped out of his hand and clattered down the corridor. It was now a couple of feet away. "Nick, shoot him."

Nick raised the Glock but was paralyzed by fear. He'd never killed anyone. He'd never been in a situation like this. But in that moment, when he was seconds away from squeezing the trigger, the soldier turned and looked at him. "Don't shoot," he said.

"Shoot him!" Emerick continued to cry out as the soldier maintained his grip on Emerick's throat.

The soldier looked back down at Emerick and said, "You're not infected?"

"Do I look like it?" Emerick asked. "Are you?"

He shook his head.

The soldier glanced at Nick again and then released his grip and rose to his feet. "I thought you were one of them," he said brushing himself off and then clutching Emerick's hand and hauling him to his feet. "I'm sorry but can't be too careful."

"Yeah, well maybe next time ask before you decide to go all python on my ass," Emerick said angrily before making his way down and scooping up his rifle.

"Why are you still here?" Nick asked lowering his weapon.

The soldier cast a nervous glance down the hallway. "We were overrun both from inside and out. It happened within hours of being here. Some of the teachers and students began to act erratic, then locals, parents I believe showed up here and wanted answers. I'm not sure if they were infected or not but arguments over their kids turned into a riot and once the shooting began, it got out of control real fast. We were in the process of loading them on to school buses to transfer to a temporary FEMA camp not far from here when it all happened. I got lost in the chaos. Dropped my gun and..." he trailed off and looked down as if embarrassed or ashamed. Nick had a sense that wasn't exactly how it played out and maybe he ran out of fear and hid. It wouldn't have been the first time he'd heard of military guys losing it in the heat of battle. Not everyone was hardened and prepared to deal with bullets flying over their heads.

"Well—" Emerick was about to say something when a loud bang down below put them all on alert.

"Quick, this way," the soldier said.

"What is your name?" Nick asked.

"Chad O'Brien." He led them into the room he'd come out of. He closed the door behind them, then opened a window, where he proceeded to climb out. "Come on," he said as they hesitated to follow. It wasn't that they didn't want to get as far away from this place as possible, it was the question of why hadn't he? If this had all taken place hours ago, why was he still here? Nick was the first to climb out. As soon as they were out, he closed the window and hunched over jogging towards a large steel vent protruding from the roof.

"Why haven't you escaped?" Emerick asked.

"It's not because I haven't wanted to leave, it's because it's damn near impossible. Let me show you." Chad took them over to the lip of the roof, which provided a view of the east side. Down below there had to have been approximately a hundred people. Some of them looked dazed and confused, others stood frozen looking ahead and mumbling to themselves.

"What the hell are they doing?"

"It's the disease. They go through different stages. It affects the memory, their anxiety and fear. In the early hours it causes some to be frozen by fear itself, others react," he said pointing to different ones lashing out at others around them. "I don't know everything about how it affects them, only what we were told and my own observations. Within twelve hours their skin and eyes change, and they become extremely violent, driven by fear itself. Seeing everything and everyone around them as a threat. Before that they are unstable, shifting back and forth between extreme fear and an unusually calm state. That's the most dangerous time. You don't know what to expect, you might not know if they're infected," he said glancing at Emerick as if apologizing without saying it.

"But the entire school can't be surrounded. We got in here on the north side."

"Yeah, maybe you lucked out, so why are you here now?"

"Well, there was..." Emerick trailed off realizing he was walking right into the obvious.

Chad pulled away. "I need to get a gun."

"You've been here all this time and you didn't search for one?"

His brow furrowed. "No, I was too busy trying to avoid them. I didn't know what the hell was going on down below. The last time I saw it, it was a bloodbath."

"Sounds like someone was scared," Emerick said rising to his feet and chuckling.

"Hey, I'm not scared of anything."

"Really? And yet it's here we find you, hiding away like a...rat!" Emerick said in a condescending tone. Chad balled his fist and took a step forward.

"Go on! Take a swing," Emerick said. "I'm in the mood for it."

"Guys. Seriously. This isn't helping. We need to find a way off this roof."

"Yeah, and go where?" Chad asked motioning with one arm to the crowd of maniacs below.

"You said the military was taking the kids to a FEMA camp. Where is it?" Emerick asked.

"Why? You want to join them? Because they will round up anyone who is showing even the slightest animosity. And right now yours is off the charts," Chad said.

Emerick scowled. "Yeah, well I have a good reason."

"He wants to find his son. A friend of mine. The guy that was on the roof."

Chad's mouth widened, a grin appearing. "Oh him? He's your son? Oh well that all makes sense now." Emerick lost it and threw a punch but Chad moved and Emerick toppled over. "Stay down!" Chad said jabbing a finger at him.

Emerick rose to his feet and brushed himself off before narrowing his eyes. "And there was me about to help you find a gun, and a way off this roof. But now you're on your own."

"Emerick," Nick said as he strolled away.

Nick glanced at Chad and shrugged. What could he do, he wasn't the one who threw the punch. Sure he was a dick for saying what he did but no one was thinking straight, especially Emerick. Nick lifted a hand to indicate to Chad to wait. Emerick was about to jump down to a separate part of the roof when Nick grabbed him by the arm. He swung around thinking it was Chad and clocked Nick in the face. He hit the ground and let out a groan.

"Oh shit. Nick. I'm sorry. I thought you were…"

"What an asshole," Chad said.

On his knees, Nick wiped blood from the corner of his mouth and waved him off as Emerick placed a hand on his back. "Just stop, Emerick. Enough. The only way out of here is to work together. You have problems with him, he has issues with you. Lay them to one side for now and just work together for fuck's sake!" Nick got up, brushed himself off, headed over to the lip of the roof and hopped down onto the adjoining building. It was about a four-foot drop. He landed hard and looked up to see both of them staring down. They glanced at each other for a second before following.

They moved quickly across the surface of the building to the south side, hopping down, and climbing up to each section of the school. It was so damn dark, and the streetlights for some reason were out, that if there were any of those freaks down there they could easily overwhelm them. Chad stopped at a window, and crouched. They were right above the gym area and he was peering through the skylight. "There's a rifle down there."

"Yeah, well it's going to stay down there," Emerick said, passing him.

Chad lifted the window and peered in. "Look, I can get it. I just need to climb down onto the beam, go across and use one of those gym ropes to make my way down. There's no one moving inside."

"We heard them enter. They're in there."

"Look, I'm not asking you to go in. Just watch my

back from the window. If you see anything, shoot it. We need that extra gun. You need my help."

There was no arguing with that but still, going back down there was a big risk. Chad looked inside again, and Emerick walked over and peered over his shoulder, satisfying his own curiosity. "Okay, it's your funeral."

Nick smirked as Chad swallowed and cautiously climbed over the edge and lowered himself down onto one of the thick steel beams. "Let's see if all that money Uncle Sam invested in you was worth it," Emerick said with his lip curling up. Chad flipped him the bird and Emerick chuckled. Nick kept an eye on the other windows in nearby buildings and watched Emerick's back while they waited.

* * *

Beads of sweat trickled down Chad's face as he shimmied along the structural beams and peered down at lifeless bodies. Fear gripped him as the memory of people losing control came flooding back in. What he hadn't told Emerick was he was right. He had fled and abandoned his post out of fear. He'd seen his buddies drop in front of his eyes; he'd seen a kid's head taken off with a shotgun, and a young girl thrown through a window. In the heat of the moment fear had overwhelmed him and he scrambled up the stairwell, petrified of dying. He'd encountered a hostile on the way up and lost his service weapon in the fight, before he'd thrown the guy over the railing. Then for hours he'd hid on the roof, his hands clasped over his ears to silence the sounds of screams. It was only when he knew he couldn't remain there that he'd ventured inside. That's when he'd heard Emerick.

Now here he was balancing forty feet in the air, his palms sweating and the blood rushing in his ears. Down below he could see a soldier face down, a rifle still in hand, and a sidearm attached to his hip. He made his way over to the ropes and was about to climb down when the gym doors opened. He glanced at Emerick, who had spotted the intruder and was preparing to take him out. Now had he been the only one that entered, he would have given him the go-ahead but three more followed straight after. *Shit,* he thought, staying as quiet as he could. Sweat was tickling his lip as each drop rolled down. He didn't dare move to wipe them away. He locked eyes with Emerick and shook his head to make it clear not to fire.

The four people wandered the gym, seemingly oblivious to each other as if confused and dazed, and just operating with a herd mentality. He couldn't see well enough from where he was whether their skin had changed or not. Slowly but surely they exited on the other side and the door swung closed.

It was now or never.

Chad wrapped his feet and hands around the thick yellow rope and slid down as fast as he could. As soon as he hit the ground he made his way over, scooped up the rifle and put the gun into his holster before relieving the soldier of ammo. No sooner had he done that than the door opened. Chad dropped to his face, lying prone on the ground. He didn't dare move or breathe. Fear rose in his chest, suffocating him as he stared into the eyes of his fallen comrade — Mark Roberts.

They had gone through boot camp together, seen two tours in the Middle East and lived in the same city. He had a wife, and a young baby. They would be devastated.

Chad heard the approaching footsteps and all he could do was lie there and not move, hoping they would pass him. Through slitted eyes he saw a pair of combat boots come into frame. They were military.

For a split second he thought it was his squad returning to collect him, until he looked up and saw one of the infected.

His movement gave away his position, and the maniac let out a scream.

Chapter 17

Three floors of apartments, and all he could do was guess which one the shooter was in. Sergio had seen the muzzle flash but with it being so dark and multiple windows on the outside of the building, it was hard to judge which door corresponded to which apartment. He knew the shooter was on the third floor but that was it. All he could do was hope they fired a few more shots at Lars. It would instantly give them away.

He entered the dingy hallway. Sick looking fluorescent lights from emergency lights flicked on and off making him feel like he was in a dance club. Darkness, then light. A constant blinking that was nauseating. He strode down the hallway stopping at each apartment and putting an ear to the unfinished wooden doors. The apartment block was a shithole, a tenant's nightmare. How landlords managed to get away with such subpar standards was a mystery. A cockroach scuttled across the worn carpeted floor, and the sound of music kicked in from an apartment further down as the smell of weed lingered in the air. It was always the same. These were the bottom feeders of society, the ones who worked the system. He couldn't stand them and the thought of ridding the earth of one of them brought him great satisfaction, especially after Lars had been shot and almost killed. He pressed on going apartment to apartment until he arrived at the one blaring music. He wasn't a gambling man but if he had to lay a bet, this was the one. Sergio noticed the peephole. So he moved to one side and banged on the door.

"Davey, is that you?" a female voice yelled out.

It caught him off guard. He struck the door again and mumbled "C'mon" in a low throaty voice. He could hear multiple locks being pulled back, followed by two chains sliding off rails before the door cracked open. Sergio reared around kicking the door wide, and knocking the occupant on their ass. It was a guy. Suddenly coming into view further inside, a woman pulled around the corner with a rifle. He had just enough time to dive out of the way before she unleashed a flurry of rounds from an AR-15. That was more firepower than he was ready to deal with and under any other circumstances he might have let it go and got the hell out of there, but all hell had broken loose in town, and the chances of the cops showing up were slim to none, so no, he wasn't going anywhere, not until he had blood.

Sergio pulled into the nearest stairwell and waited with his back to the wall.

He glanced out and the door was now closed. "Sonofabitch!"

Slipping back into the hallway he made his way down and listened carefully. On the other side of the door he could hear the guy groaning. "My fucking nose. He busted my nose."

"Get up, grab your rifle and stop being a pussy."

He smirked. She obviously wore the pants.

Sergio took advantage of the moment and aimed at the door, and fired four shots through it in rapid succession before he got out of the way. Loud cries echoed and he knew he'd landed at least one shot. The question was whether they were both injured.

That was soon answered with multiple rounds tearing through the door and peppering the wall across from him. He smiled, waiting patiently for that bitch to come out. As he waited, crouched on the ground, fully expecting her to appear, a door opened up several apartments down and an old man walked out, his eyes red and skin weathered. He turned his head and gave Sergio an absent look before shuffling in his direction.

What the hell was he doing?

Anyone in their right mind would have stayed inside.

More rounds erupted.

Though he didn't care for many, this guy had obviously lost his marbles. "Get back. Go back into your apartment," Sergio yelled waving him back. But he paid no attention. His expression was stoic, unmoved by the flurry of rounds. Like someone sleep walking, totally oblivious to what was going on around him, he pressed on until he stepped into the fatal funnel. His body shook, and looked like it was convulsing as round after round tore through him, sending a mist of blood over the wall.

Insane. Utterly insane, he thought.

He shook his head and was about to pull back to the stairwell when he saw out the corner of his eye someone rushing him. He turned just in time to avoid a lunatic wielding a heavy fire extinguisher. It missed his head by inches. Sergio didn't hesitate, he unloaded a round into his skull and snuffed his lights out.

Had that been the only one, he would have turned his focus back to the apartment but it wasn't. A woman screamed coming at him with two knives in her hands. Her raggedy hair hung low over her dirty face. All she was wearing was a bra and panties. Her skin looked like it was melting off her.

"Ahhh," he yelled as he toppled back to avoid the blades as she slashed the air. He hit the ground and rolled as she came down, driving the tip of the second knife into the carpet. Sergio whipped around and unloaded a round into her neck, followed by one more to the gut. He backed up, shock setting in. He had no qualms about killing but this made him feel like a fish out of water. What the hell had everyone been drinking?

Scrambling to his feet, he decided to cut his losses and get the hell out before he found himself out of ammo and fighting off a horde of these assholes. He took a few steps and stepped over the woman when the bitch with the AR-15 emerged on the other side of the glass divider. Their eyes locked and as if they knew exactly what the other was thinking, they raised their guns. Neither one of them squeezed the trigger though.

He wasn't sure why.

He could have killed her in that instant, she could have done the same but then it hit him. Maybe she thought he was one of them. Perhaps she wasn't randomly picking them off, she was defending her turf and now, only now after she'd witnessed him kill one of those freaks, she was seeing him a different light.

With one hand opened, he reached for the door and pulled it back holding it ajar with his foot. Slowly they both lowered their weapons.

"You're not one of them, are you?" she said.

He shook his head. "No."

Her eyes dropped, as did her weapon to her side. "I'm sorry…"

Before she uttered the words or could react, Sergio raised his Glock and fired a round into her head. She slumped to the floor and he spat on her body. "You speak too much," he said before making his way back to Lars. A pool of blood seeped over the edge of the steps behind him turning the steps into a mini stream of red.

Chapter 18

Brody shouldered the cabin door, struggling to keep it closed from opposing pressure on the other side. The woman clutched her baby and cowered in a corner sobbing her heart out. "Push that table over here," he yelled over his shoulder. She glanced at it for a second then shook her head. "Lady, if you don't help me now we both die. Now do it!" It was getting harder to keep the door closed. If he could just get it shut, he could lock it but he'd barely managed to close the door when he felt them forcing their way in. The woman set her baby down on the ground and hurried to a table. Just as she began to shift it, a brick shattered the window landing a few feet from her baby. She screamed and pulled back, fear controlling her as she returned and scooped up her child. Brody reached around for his Glock and fired two rounds through the door. A sudden release in pressure and he was able to close it and slam the bolt home.

Suddenly someone ran at the window and crashed through it. Glass scattered, and the intruder rolled across the floor.

Brody turned and fired a round into the stranger's head, killing the intruder instantly. He backed up and unleashed several more shots through the door as more people pounded on it. A loud crash above them, and both of them looked up and realized people on the roof. Brody fired into different areas hoping to get them off. The woman with the child screamed again as someone tried to get through the now open window. The glass was cutting their hands but it didn't seem to faze them. A guy got half his body in before Brody ended his life. He went to unload another round as a pane of glass to the left shattered but he'd run out of rounds. He pulled his second magazine, released the other, palmed the next into place and continued his tirade of rounds to keep them at bay. Anyone in their right mind might have backed up but these people seemed unfazed by the danger of being shot.

He knew if they kept this up he would soon be out of ammo and even if he could hold them at bay with the metal rod, his chances of being infected would increase. He'd kept his distance from the woman and the child out of fear of contracting the contagion.

Rounds echoed one after the other as he held the tide at bay.

Right then he heard the sound of an engine, and rock music blaring out loudly. A flood of light lit up the faces of the infected briefly before an RV plowed through them. It was Gottman. A wave of relief washed over him as he watched the RV accelerate for a second time at the mad crowd. The sound of bodies bouncing off metal dominated until the RV squealed to a stop just beyond the shattered window.

"Come on, chief! We don't have all day," Gottman shouted as he extended his hand out the driver's window and took potshots with his handgun.

Brody motioned to the woman to go but she shook her head. He wasn't going to grab her, not after he'd seen that infected woman coddling her child. And as he looked at her, he had to wonder if she was now infected. "Lady, do you want to live?"

She glanced at the RV and the people who were still trying to get in and she nodded.

"Okay, I'll head out first and clear the way then you follow. You understand?"

He was aware that she might be infected but there was the slim possibility that she wasn't. He wouldn't know for sure until Sorenson looked her over. For now he would keep his distance and if he could get her into the RV, she would stay at the back away from them.

"Chief!" Gottman yelled again.

The sound of his gun erupting forced Brody into action. He hopped up onto the surrounding granite counter and fired a few rounds through at the assholes close to the window before leaping out and unloading even more. "Come on!" he shouted to the woman as he opened the RV door and beckoned her to hurry. She clambered up with her baby and stared out, hesitating to jump. Under any other conditions he would have had her throw the baby out and he would have caught it, but there was no way in hell he was going near that bundle of joy.

"Lady, I'm telling you now. If you don't move ass..."

She jumped and Brody hopped into the RV expecting her to follow but as she staggered to get her footing, four of the infected rushed her. Brody unloaded one round taking out one of them but then he was out of ammo. By the time he released the mag and loaded another one in, it was too late. They had dived on her and the child and she disappeared below the angry mob. His stomach dropped as he slammed the door on the RV closed and Gottman tore out of there. The dull sound of people being hit by the RV and the bump as wheels rolled over them was sickening. All he could think about was that poor mother and her child. What if they hadn't been infected? He pushed the thought from his mind and made his way to the front and slumped into the passenger seat. Gottman navigated to the far end of the lot, and swerved in front of the tree line where Sorenson and the others were waiting. Brody opened the door and they piled in. He cast a glance back at the rec room in the distance and saw only flames licking up into the night sky.

Not everyone could be saved.

* * *

Before the infected man could attack Chad, a single bullet from Emerick's rifle exploded his skull. Chad scrambled to his feet just as several more infected crashed through the gym doors. "Move it!" Emerick yelled before unleashing round after round to hold them at bay. Chad clasped the rope and began to climb. The muscles in his arms burned like fire. Instantly, his thoughts went back to boot camp. He'd never been too good at the obstacle course, and many times his buddies had to help him over the wall, but now he was ascending that rope like a monkey. Below, the maniacs that had managed to elude Emerick's shots gave chase, clambering up the rope behind him. Chad glanced down for a second then kept going. He was nearly at the top when he felt a hand clasp his boot. He peered down to find a young kid hanging on for dear life. He yanked his leg free and then drove his heel hard into the kid's face, knocking him off the rope. His body hit the ground, taking out some of the others that had crowded and were in pursuit. As soon as he made it onto the wide beam he scuttled along the top with all the prowess of a cougar. It was only when he reached the window and Emerick extended a hand to pull him up did he look back and see the aftermath. One quick tug and he was safe. He hit the roof and rolled onto his back breathing hard while Emerick continued to take out those who had made it onto the steel beam.

"Save your bullets," Chad said. "We're going to need every one of them."

* * *

While Emerick was covering Chad, Nick had been scanning the perimeter and trying to find a safe way off. A large abandoned yellow school bus was parked near the south side, its doors partly open as if the military had considered using it but at the last moment opted out.

While it might not be operational, its proximity to the school meant they could easily scale down one of the drainpipes and launch themselves onto the top. He hurried back, scaling up the structure of one side of the school to find Emerick and Chad making their way over to him.

"You survived," he said acting surprised.

"Barely," Emerick said casting a glance at Chad. "What have you found?"

He brought them up to speed and they went over to the lip of the school and took a look for themselves. "Anyone in that?" Emerick asked.

"Looks empty to me. Haven't seen any movement," Nick said.

Chad kept looking over his shoulder as if expecting to see more of those lunatics.

"What do you say?" Nick asked.

"We don't have much choice. Though I wish I knew where Angela went."

"You told her to get out of there if they encountered

trouble. She's probably long gone by now."

"Great," Emerick said climbing over the lip and testing out the strength of the drainpipe. He gave it a good shake. "Seems secure enough. Let's do this."

One at time they climbed down and hopped onto the bus. They stayed low and scanned for movement. There were a few silhouettes of people going in and out of the school but beyond that the coast seemed clear. Nick went to the front end and peered over the edge into the bus. It was dark inside but it looked good. He was hoping to see if there were any keys inside but unless one of them risked entering they wouldn't be able to tell. "Look, I'm gonna go down."

"No, you'll stay here," Emerick said.

"I'm not a kid."

"I think your father would differ," he replied. "Besides, if there's no keys in there I don't think you know how to hot-wire a car, now do you?"

"Actually I do."

He chuckled then stared blankly at him. "Kid, I've

been alive long enough to learn a thing or two but you're telling me you know how to start this beast?"

Nick nodded.

Emerick looked at Chad for moral support but he wasn't getting it.

Chad remained quiet observing his surroundings. He looked comfortable with a rifle in hand. Realizing Emerick had few options, Nick took over the situation. "All right. If you see anyone, and I mean anyone, approach this bus, take them out. Do you understand? As soon as I'm inside I will shut the doors and check the ignition. It's going to take me a few minutes to get this sucker started if I have to hot-wire."

"I don't even want to know how you learned," Emerick replied as Nick prepared to slide down the front of the bus and go in the side. They did one last check before he gave a nod and quickly slid down the hood and onto the ground. Within less than twenty seconds he was inside the bus. He twisted and closed the main doors before pulling out his phone and turning on the flashlight portion. He shone it down the aisle and swallowed hard before sliding into the driver's seat and checking. *Oh, great. No keys.*

Now he wasn't lying when he said he knew how to hot-wire. A close buddy of his old man had shown him a few summers back on a '67 Chevy. But that was an old beast, a car, not a bus and certainly not a modern one. Still, how hard could it be? He heard Emerick ask if he was okay. He went over to the doors and yelled up, "Yeah. Just watch my back."

Nick went to work.

One of the things that struck him when he was shown was that it was nothing like the movies. They'd always made it look so easy. Tear out a bottom portion below the steering wheel, snap wires and twist together and bingo you'd be up and running. Nope. When he was shown, the guy had used a hammer, a flathead screwdriver, a Phillips screwdriver, insulated gloves, insulated tape, wire cutters and strippers. He had none of that shit. So he was working on a prayer and winging it.

He got down beneath the wheel. It stunk like old farts, and grease. Grime covered his hands immediately as he shone the light underneath and tried to figure out what he was dealing with. Originally his father's pal had pounded a flathead screwdriver into the ignition and turned it like a key. That alone could often make a vehicle start if it was an old model. Beyond that it required removing the panels from above and below the steering column. Once the plastic panels were removed, the ignition cylinder was exposed along with the wires running to it. From there he had to identify the battery and starter wires which was usually easy to figure out as the two red wires handled power and the brown ones dealt with the starter. Next came putting insulated gloves on, cutting the power wires, stripping the ends and twisting together. At this point the lights, radio and other items in the car would switch on. Then it was a case of doing the same with the brown ones. The tricky part was doing it without gloves, which meant potentially exposing himself to a live current that would shock him. Once the two ends were touched, the car would start, and then the key was to tape the ends to avoid getting shocked while driving. Right now he would just be glad to get the damn panel off. He was yanking hard on it but it wouldn't budge. He got up and went over to the doors, pulled the handle to open them and then called up. "Chad. You got a knife?"

"What?" Emerick said. "I thought you knew how to do this?"

Nick ignored him. "Chad?"

A second later a blade dropped and Nick scooped it up. He closed the doors and returned, this time armed to rip that sucker off and get it started. He squeezed back into the spot and dug the tip of the blade in and jiggled it around until he snapped the plastic away from the screws and the panel dropped. There before him were all the wires. "All right. You can do this. How hard can this be?"

As he began to shine the light on the wires and figure out which wire was which, he heard movement in the back of the bus. He stopped and listened. Nothing. He continued then heard a shuffle again. He thought it was Chad or Emerick moving around on the top but when it happened a third time it was clear it was coming from inside.

Chapter 19

Lynch had been at the temporary FEMA camp located somewhere between Fort Davis and Alpine, just east of Highway 118, when she got word of the breach. She'd been waiting on the students arriving from Marfa when the call came in. Major Tim Brown who was on scene at the time contacted her by way of a secure line. He was yelling, and the sound of a chopper could be heard nearby. "It's out of control."

"What?" Lynch replied as she rose from a table where she'd been briefed about several incidents further afield. One of her biggest fears was that it had spread before they'd arrived, or that someone would escape before they could implement a cordon sanitaire. Tim's voice kept cutting in and out. It didn't help that he was shouting orders to some soldiers at the same time he was on the phone with her. But it was what followed next that worried her. The sound of a rapid succession of gunfire and the cries of men.

"Major. What the hell is going on?" she yelled pacing back and forth in a makeshift tent. It was one of many inside a fenced perimeter currently being patrolled by armed guards. The line went dead. She tried to get him back on the phone but he never picked up. She had several contacts in Marfa and in Alpine — different soldiers that were overseeing checkpoints. She tried them but got no answer. Lynch went over to the door.

"Private Johnson."

A young guy with buzz cut hair, and a bounce to his step hurried over. "Yes, colonel?"

"Find Lieutenant Mosley."

He saluted and shot off. Mosley was in charge of overseeing the work at the FEMA camp. If there was a shit situation that the US military was behind, he was one of the crew sent in to clean it up. He was also in contact with a team that was in Marfa. Lynch didn't want to get too worried. It wasn't the first time she'd heard gunfire. Since this had kicked off they'd all had several close brushes with death. It was the nature of the work they were in. While she rarely was on the front line, dealing with immediate threats, the major was. His track record in the military, four tours overseas and medals of honor, was the reason they had worked together for the past eleven years. She handled logistics, he handled enforcement.

She made her way back into the tent and resumed her position at the desk, looking at the recent update on her laptop that had come in from hospitals in the Texas region, and farther afield. FEMA and the World Health Organization were monitoring anyone who showed up in emergency rooms for symptoms related to the amygdala syndrome. Within a span of two days they had seen nine incidents, two potential fatalities and four people showing symptoms within four different states. They had managed to contain the infected and clear those who came in contact with them but that didn't mean it hadn't spread further. The thought of it going nationwide, or worse, global, was horrifying. If they didn't manage to reel this in and fast, the media would soon be all over it, fear would spread and it would be out of their control.

"You wanted to see me, colonel?"

She glanced up to see Mosley standing in the entranceway. He was an overbearing, barrel chested man with a scar across his left eye. She'd never asked him how he got it but figured it was one of many battle scars. He smelled like cheap cologne and had this gaze that made her feel uneasy.

"When was your last update from Marfa?" she asked.

"Several hours ago. They were making preparations to board the infected onto buses and escort them here."

"Get them on the line."

His brow furrowed but he didn't question it. He retrieved a satellite phone from a pocket on his chest and made the attempt. The sound of static played out, then a desperate voice. "Lieutenant, we had a breach."

As soon as Lynch heard that her stomach sank.

"Where are you?" Mosley asked.

The soldier continued, "We were unable to leave town,

our platoon has been attacked. Fires are raging here, and we are seeking cover in the Palace Theater. We need backup. This is spreading fast."

"Roger that."

Mosley glanced at Lynch and she placed a hand against her forehead.

"We can handle this," he said as if that was reassuring.

"And if you can't? Do you know the firestorm this will cause? The president is expecting good news. Now I have to tell him that we might have a nationwide pandemic on our hands."

"The upside is that it kills the infected within seventy-two hours."

Her eyebrows shot up. "Oh, well that's great then. Let's just sit back on our laurels and wait for the nation to die out, shall we?"

Mosley sighed and looked around the small enclosure. It wasn't much, just a military-issued cot for a bed, a desk and chair and that was it. "We can send in more soldiers."

"And risk the chance of them getting infected? No, we

have sent in enough. Either your soldiers can deal with this or we will have to look for an alternative."

"Alternative?" he asked cocking his head. "You mean…"

She didn't want to say it as it was a last resort for worst-case scenarios but if it came down to a few thousand lives vs. seven billion, they would implement it.

Lynch took a deep breath. "I need to talk to the president and FEMA before we go down that path. In the meantime I want an update every half hour on the situation as it unfolds. Is the perimeter still secure?"

"I'll find out."

"God I hope so because Alpine sounds like they aren't faring much better."

"The major?"

"I can't get through to him."

"Ma'am, let me take in a small team to at least assess the situation. Right now we are dealing with unknowns and little information."

"How about you start with a drone? A team goes in

only if you can come up with a solution that will save our troops. I'm not having any suicide missions. I'm already taking the full brunt of this. It's a complete mess."

* * *

A shot of cold fear went through Nick as he crawled out from underneath the steering column and peered down the aisle. He reached for the Glock and squeezed it tight, a lump forming in his throat. "Whoever is there you better come out."

There was no response.

He considered leaving the bus but maybe it was just his imagination playing tricks on him. Since this whole thing had kicked off, his senses were heightened and his mind had gone into overdrive thinking that even the slightest sound was a threat. He swallowed hard as he slowly walked from the front to the back of the bus, turning and raking the barrel of the gun from the left to right in quick succession.

"This is your last chance."

Still nothing.

The hairs on his arms rose. It felt like he was living inside his own horror movie. With every step he could feel fear creeping up in his chest causing his mouth to go dry, and his palms to sweat.

By the time he made it to the last four rows of seats he had convinced himself that the noise was nothing more than a concoction of a runaway mind. That was until he saw him cowering, his face hidden by darkness. His body was shaking. Words spilled out. "Please. Please. Don't shoot."

"Jasper?" Nick frowned. "Jasper McDermott?"

The boy looked up at him as Nick took out his cell and cast the glow of its light over his face. Jasper was a short, pudgy guy, with cropped ginger hair, the kind of kid that had few friends, kept to himself but was exceptionally smart. He wore a pair of glasses that always looked two sizes too small for him, and his clothes looked like they'd been pulled out of a bargain bin at a thrift store. When he'd pass him in class, he'd always remember him smelling like mothballs. The little that he knew about him came from a talk he gave in school about how he spent his summer. While other kids talked about going on vacations, or hanging out at the mall, or gaming, he would talk about studying and helping his father who was a scientist. Although a few of the kids would chuckle when he spoke, Nick couldn't help but be intrigued.

"How the hell did you get out?"

"They led us out to the buses, and I rolled underneath when someone was giving the soldiers trouble."

Nick smiled then it faded as he began to think about the infected. "Have you been in contact with anyone who's infected?"

He shook his head. As much as he wanted to believe him, he didn't want to risk his life so he took a few steps back. "Get up," he said keeping the gun on him.

"Are you going to kill me?"

"I want to see you."

He took a few more steps back as Jasper rose and squeezed out into the aisle. Nick shone the light directly in his eyes causing him to squint and blink hard. His skin looked normal, eyes fine. Nick frowned.

"How long have you been in here?"

"However long it's been since they began loading us onto buses."

"So you saw it all play out. The breakdown?"

"I didn't see it. I heard it. I haven't been on this bus the whole time. I managed to hide back in the school for a while but then I ran in to a few of those things."

"People you mean?"

"Those aren't people."

"Well they aren't things. They're people. They die and they don't get up."

"You've killed one?"

"No, but my friends have."

Jasper's brow furrowed. "Friends?"

Nick pointed to the roof.

They could hear the sound of Chad and Emerick moving around. "It's Devan's father and some soldier. Look, wait here. I need to tell them about you."

Nick turned to leave but he stopped when Jasper said,

"No. There is no need. I'm fine."

"I know that. But you want to get out of here, right?"

He nodded.

"Then they need to know. Look, it's cool. Just wait here."

Nick wandered back to the front of the bus looking over his shoulder every so often to make sure he didn't bolt. There was something that unnerved him. "Hey, guys, guys!"

"What is it?" Emerick said.

"We have company."

"Where?"

"Inside," he replied looking back at Jasper. "It's a kid. A student from my school."

"Don't go near him."

"I'm not. I mean, I haven't. What do you want to do?"

"Just keep your distance. Get this damn bus started. This place is giving me the heebie-jeebies."

Nick nodded and looked back at Jasper who was glancing out the window and tapping his finger against the seat. "Look, I have something to do. While I think you're okay, I would prefer if you kept your distance until we get this started."

"You know how to do that?" Jasper asked.

"Somewhat."

"Somewhat? You don't sound very confident."

Nick frowned. "It's a new vehicle."

He slid back under and continued to examine the wires. While he was doing it he heard footsteps approaching. He slid out before they got too close. "Do you not listen?"

"I just thought I might be able to help."

"If you could, you would have started this already."

"I don't know how to drive."

"Then how would you know how to hot-wire a car?"

"How do you?" Jasper asked.

"I was shown."

Jasper shrugged. "Just thought I might be able to help but I'll just stay here."

"Yeah, you do that," Nick replied, raising an eyebrow

and getting back underneath. He sighed. This was nothing like what his father's buddy showed him. What the hell were all these wires?

"How we doing?" Jasper asked.

"Fine," Nick said trying to make out that he had this in hand.

"You sure you don't need a hand?"

"No. I got this." He stared blankly at the wires and shone the light on them cursing under his breath. Why did manufacturers have to make everything so damn hard? He grumbled and pulled at the wires. Did he cut this one? The last thing he wanted was to get a shock and be flopping around like a fish. He'd never live that one down with Emerick.

"You know there is an easier way."

"Jasper. Can't you see I'm working here?"

Jasper poked his head around and Nick backed up. "What did I say?"

"Okay, okay." He backed up with his hand up. "I'm just saying that I think you could use my help."

Nick groaned and even though he didn't want to admit he couldn't do it, he'd reached the end of his rope. "Fine. Let's hear it."

Expecting to hear Jasper reel off some goofy idea that he'd probably seen in a movie, he was surprised when he heard the jangle of keys and saw them come into view. "These should do it."

Nick crawled out telling him to back up. "Hold on a minute. You've had the keys all this time?"

"Well yeah."

"And you didn't think to tell me?"

"I tried. I offered my help but you…"

"I know what I said. Geesh." He shook his head and went to take them then stopped short. "Maybe you should put it in the ignition and turn it over." He moved out of the way and let Jasper take a seat and try a few of the keys until he found the right one. A few seconds later the engine rumbled to life and he slid back out.

"Hey, the kid did it!" Emerick cried out.

Both of them looked up and Jasper said, "I won't tell

them."

Nick offered back a thin smile. "I think they'll know."

They heard the metal above them bounce as they hopped down onto the hood and Nick opened the door so they could board. "Well, kid. Maybe you aren't useless," Emerick muttered as he got on board. He stared at Jasper.

"Emerick. This is Jasper. Jasper, Emerick and Chad."

"We're not a couple."

"I didn't say you were." Nick grinned as Chad boarded the bus.

Chapter 20

Twelve minutes past one in the morning. The red numbers flashed before her eyes as Jenna blinked. Her head was throbbing, mostly her jaw. It felt like she'd been through intense dental surgery or gone three rounds with a professional fighter. Her head was resting on a pillow, and her surroundings were dark. She groaned a little and rolled to take in the sight of the room. A small flashlight was illuminating just a fraction of the cramped space. She'd been tucked under blankets and at first she thought she was alone until she glanced off to her left. Sitting in a rocking chair, with his head slumped to one side was Brody. He was asleep. A handgun was resting on his lap. She didn't recognize where she was. Drapes were closed but a small amount of moonlight filtered through. At the far end of the bed was a dresser with a mirror, and to the right a closet.

She turned to reach for a glass of water on the bedside

table, and accidentally overextended her reach and knocked it off the side. It hit the hardwood floor and smashed startling Brody awake. He grasped for his gun and stretched it out like he was about to shoot. That's when he locked eyes with her.

"Jenna?"

"Sorry, I knocked over the glass."

He glanced down and then his face relaxed. He rocked forward in his chair and reached for her hand, gripping it tightly. "How are you feeling?"

"Rough. Where are we?"

"Ray Gottman's house."

"Officer Gottman?"

He nodded.

A flood of memories hit her. The hospital. The lockdown. The gunfire. Then being attacked. That was her last memory. She reached up and touched her face. It felt swollen.

"You're missing a tooth but besides that you were damn lucky he didn't kill you. Gottman shot the guy before he turned your head into pulp."

Her mouth went slack. Gratitude. Embarrassment. A whole range of emotions welled up in her. She lay back and gazed up at the ceiling. There was a fan but it wasn't on. "Electricity?"

"Appears to be down. Think it has something to do with what's happening in the town." Brody got up and headed for the door. "I'll get you another drink and see if he has a broom to sweep up the glass. Be careful and just stay put."

"Brody."

He stopped with his hand on the doorknob. "Yeah?"

"Thank you for coming."

She caught a smile on his face before he headed out without saying anything. A few minutes later he returned with another glass of water, some ice for her face and a pan and brush. She took a sip and watched him as he swept up the shards. "What's the situation like out there?"

"Bad. The whole damn town has gone to shits. Sorenson says it's out of control and the best we can do is to try and get out of town before the military acts."

"Acts?"

He looked up at her from a crouched position. "They are killing people, Jenna. They are shooting first and not asking questions. There is no Internet. No TV. No electricity right now in town. They are going to wipe out anyone who they think is a threat and the problem is, until a person's skin and eyes change, there is no way to determine if they are infected. They aren't asking. They've been told to kill on sight. At least that was the last thing Sorenson heard before he lost contact with those in charge."

Jenna set her glass down.

"Have you heard from Nick?"

He shook his head. "Gottman and I are planning to head to Marfa and see if we can locate him."

"I'll go with you."

"Jenna, you're not up to going. You've been out for several hours. You took a hard blow to the head. You should probably rest up."

"Our son is out there."

"Yeah, and I will find him but it's not safe. You'll be fine here. All of you."

"The others are here?"

"Sorenson, and the group you were with when we found you."

She stared back at him. "Why did you risk your life for me?"

Brody stopped sweeping and took a seat on the edge of the bed. He gazed down at the ground. "Look, Jenna, I know I haven't been the ideal husband. I know that losing Will crushed both of our spirits but I never gave up on us."

"So you're saying it's my fault that I left?"

"I didn't say that. Look, can we just for once not argue?"

Her eyes narrowed for a second then she nodded. Brody continued.

"Losing Will was the hardest thing I have ever been through. I didn't think I was going to make it, to be honest. There were days when I just wanted to slip out of this world as the pain was too much but I had you, and Nick to think about."

"You never spoke to me about it, Brody. I wanted to talk about it."

"I know you did."

"Then why wouldn't you?"

"Because it hurt too damn much," he shot back. "And would it really have changed anything? Will would still be dead. We would still have to get up every day and go on with our lives. I thought the best way forward was for me to bury myself in work. To just avoid thinking about it."

"But look what that's done."

He looked at her. He knew she was trying to say it was his fault. That he had somehow driven her to leave him by becoming cold and emotionally unattached but that wasn't the truth. Okay, maybe it was to some extent but the responsibility for Will's death wasn't only his burden to carry. All three of them had to deal with it and they all dealt with it in different ways.

"Jenna. I don't think we are ever going to see eye to eye on it. How you handle things is different from how I do."

She looked away and stared off towards the window. "Did you sign the papers?"

Her words lingered in the air for a minute or two. Just dead space. Nothing said between them until Brody uttered, "No."

"Why not?"

He took a deep breath and looked up at the ceiling. "Because every time I hold that pen I keep thinking about all the good times with you. Twenty-four years is a long time to be with someone, Jenna. It wasn't all bad, was it?"

She shook her head.

"I could have signed it. Put it behind me and moved on but I know I would have regretted not trying."

"We can't go back to the way it was, Brody. Having you distant and cold hurts too much."

He frowned. "And what about you?"

He was quick to turn it around on her. She closed her

eyes and counted to ten in her head to prevent herself from arguing. He had a point but it didn't help the situation. She knew she had her own baggage. "I know I haven't made it easy for you." She shook her head and a tear welled up in her eye and rolled down her cheek, landing in her mouth and leaving a salty taste. "I just didn't think you wanted me around anymore."

He turned towards her and placed his hand on hers and gave it a squeeze. She pulled it out from under his. It wasn't that she didn't want to feel his touch but it was painful to open up and be vulnerable. They'd spent so much time apart that she'd become accustomed to what it felt like. There was a sense of safety. She didn't have to argue. She didn't have to justify her reasons. She only had to think about Nick and herself. The thought of it being anything but that again scared her.

Jenna heard Brody sigh heavily before he rose from the bed.

"Look, I don't know what the future holds for us, Jenna. All I know right now is our kid is out there and

I'm going to find him. If we make it out of this alive and you still want me to sign those papers I will." He walked over to the door and placed a hand on the knob. "But know this. I won't do it because I want it to be over. I'll do it because you do."

With that said he walked out leaving her in the wake of his words.

She felt another shot of pain go through her, though this time it wasn't physical, it was deep in the heart. Like an old wound being torn back open. A wound she had convinced herself had healed. It hadn't. It was still as fresh as the day she walked out the door. Jenna would eventually decide on what she wanted to do but not right now. All that mattered was finding Nick. Besides, she was exhausted and in too much pain. She reached across and took another sip of her drink before closing her eyes.

* * *

Loud cries echoed in the room as Lars hobbled in.

Sergio swept the table clean of tools before helping Lars onto it. The closest medical place they could find was Alpine Veterinary Clinic on the west side of town. He would have taken him to the hospital but the roads were blocked by military, and fires raged, and violence seemed to be occurring in the northern area of the town more than elsewhere. Besides, it was the only place he knew.

"Why the hell did you bring me here?" Lars said.

"Oh shut your griping. It's better than letting you bleed out."

"I'm not an animal."

"That's debatable," Sergio retorted.

He'd known him a long time and he wasn't going to let him bleed out in the middle of the streets. They had to have something at the clinic for pain. He'd had two animals. Dogs. They were the only animals he really cared about. They were loyal, unlike that piece of trash Violet. The last one had passed away a year earlier from cancer. Just arriving at the vet's reminded him of the pain of losing that dog.

"Keep your hand on the wound while I try to find something."

The place was empty but the cupboards were full of meds, syringes, bandages and all kinds of equipment that might have worked in an animal. Sergio searched for a scalpel. He planned to remove the bullet and sew the wound up. He had never done it before and had no idea if it would work but desperate situations called for extreme measures and it couldn't get much worse. Blood was covering the steel table Lars was lying on. He'd tied off the leg to slow the bleeding but it would only last so long. Lars' skin had already drained of color. If he didn't get the bullet out and stitch it up he might not make it through the night.

"Sergio, I'm sure you're not supposed to remove the bullet."

"You want to bleed out?"

"If we remove it I stand a greater chance of bleeding out. That bullet might be the only thing standing between me and death."

"Listen to you. You've already given up."

"I have not given up. I'm just saying, I think I read

somewhere you are supposed to leave it in and get to a doctor."

Sergio waved his arms in a theatrical manner. "Well look around you, Einstein, do you see a doctor? It's either this, or we leave it in. You decide," he said taking out a scalpel and then pulling out his cigarette lighter and heating the end.

"What the fuck are you doing?"

"Making sure it's sterile."

"Dear God. Why don't you just put a bullet in me?"

"Stop whining."

Sergio had no idea what the hell he was doing. He was no medic. He didn't sit around watching videos on bullet removal. But he had watched Rambo, and seen him stitch up a wound. It couldn't be that far from reality, could it? "Right now this is going to hurt bad." He reached across and grabbed a towel on the counter and stuck it in Lars' mouth. "Bite down on that and just know when you wake up, it will all be over."

Lars spat it out. "That's what I'm afraid of. Come on,

Sergio. There has to be some kind of general anesthetic for dogs here. Find some."

"All right. Shut up." He put the scalpel down and continued searching. It took him a while but he soon found what appeared to be glue that was used for wounds. He returned with a bowl of warm water and a cloth and used some scissors to open up his jeans to expose the wound. "Shit, that is gnarly," Sergio said as he began to dab at it with the cloth and clean it up. Each time he touched it more blood came out. "I've got to get in there."

"Can't we just leave it in? I've heard of army guys with bullets still in them."

"You want lead poisoning?"

"I want to stay alive."

"And you will. Relax."

He raised the scalpel and Lars shook his head. "No. No. I'll leave it in. Just glue the damn thing shut and I'll take care of it later."

"You sure?"

"Yeah. Just leave it," Lars replied.

"It's your funeral."

Lars' brow furrowed.

"A figure of speech," Sergio said, correcting himself and then smiling. He released a few drops of glue around the outside of the wound and squeezed it gently together. Within a matter of seconds it had dried. He checked to see if the wound would pull apart as easily as it had before and it wouldn't. He'd just finished sealing it up and wiping clean his leg when he heard a noise, like a plastic crate being knocked over. Sergio spun around and looked towards the rear of the building. They'd come in through the front after smashing a window. The only thing that was providing light was their cell phones, which were on the counter with the flashlight portion on. Sergio scooped his up and grabbed his handgun off the counter. "Stay here."

"Sergio," Lars said gripping him.

"You'll be fine. Just wait here."

Moving through the darkness, Sergio's chest rose and

fell fast as his pulse sped up. He walked down a short hallway and reached a door. He swallowed hard and held the gun out as he used the tip of his boot to push it open. It took him into another room that smelled like damp dog. That's when he saw a German shepherd inside a crate. Its big brown eyes looked up at him. It let out a whine and he walked over and crouched down beside it. "Hey, you scared the shit out of me. For a second, I thought..."

No sooner had the words come out of his mouth than he heard movement off to his right in the dark. Sergio wheeled around just in time to see what looked like a worker for the veterinarian, a female, coming towards him. She wasn't moving fast but had this wild look on her face, and a needle in her hand. The dog whined, then barked. He didn't hesitate; Sergio raised the gun and fired a round. It struck her and knocked her to the ground. He breathed a sigh of relief and looked at the dog. He cast a glance around the room and got up to make sure there was no one else in the rear. He walked past the woman and shone the light around into the darkened corners before returning to let the dog out. There was a whole bunch of crates in there; all of the others were empty. Just as he passed the woman, she bolted upright and jammed the needle into the back of his leg. He let out a scream and fired a round into her skull finishing her off.

"Ah fuck," he said as he extracted the needle and tossed it. He went over and released the dog and it padded out brushing its head up against his leg. "Hey boy, come on, let's get you out of here." They made their way back into the next room where Lars was sitting upright, an expression of concern on his face.

"You okay?"

"Oh yeah, just dandy. Some mad bitch just stabbed me with a needle."

Lars looked down at the dog. "You picked up a stray?"

He nodded. Sergio crouched and pulled the dog's collar around. There was no name on it. "You look like a Baxter."

"What do you think is going on, Sergio?"

"With?"

"Everyone freaking out. The military?"

"Well it's safe to say this isn't some new recruitment initiative," he said before grinning and running his fingers through Baxter's hair. "Who knows but one thing is for sure, they aren't zombies. Those I've killed don't get back up again. That woman out the back was playing dead. Which tells me these assholes are smart. They haven't lost their minds totally. But what's going on up there, is anyone's guess. That guy that took a swing at you looked more terrified than he did angry."

Lars looked down at his leg and swung it off the table and tried to stand on it. It buckled a little and he winced as he tried to support himself using the counter.

"You'll need to lay off that for a while."

"Where are we going?"

"I don't know right now but we can't stay here."

"And we can't stay outside. Those fucking people are unstable."

Sergio nodded. "Unstable. You got that right. Look,

the way I see it, the military moves into this town, sets up roadblocks and locks down the hospital, so it's got to be some form of pandemic. There have been a whole lot of people acting weird since earlier today. So whatever it is, it's spreading and fast."

"So it's contagious then?"

"Of course. How many people were acting normal when we left? And look at the way things are now. That's a short window. Twelve hours at the most."

"What if we're infected?"

"Nah."

"No, I'm serious, Sergio. What if we are?"

"Well then there isn't shit we can do about it."

Sergio rose and went to cross the room when Lars grabbed him by the arm. "If anything happens to me. You know, if I contract whatever this is; promise me you'll end me. I don't want to go out like that."

"Hey, I'll end you now if you don't stop whining like a bitch."

They both grinned as he returned to help Lars up.

"You think we just stay here the night? It might be safer. Besides, my leg hurts real bad. I could use some time to let it heal. By daylight maybe we can figure out what to do then. You know, reassess," Lars added.

"Maybe. We'll see."

Sergio wasn't sure about anything but one thing he wasn't going to do was sit around hoping the military would leave. If they had gone to all the trouble to show up and quarantine the town, the chances of them letting all the residents leave twenty-four hours later were slim to none.

Chapter 21

Emerick knew it was bad when he saw the overturned school bus, and the tires in flames. They were going east on Lincoln Street in the hopes of heading to Alpine and up to the location of the FEMA camp when they found the road blocked.

An eighteen-wheeler had barreled into the side of the school bus, knocking it clear off the road and overturning it. The front half of the bus was embedded in the First Christian Church, a stunning, large white building that was just across from the Presidio County Courthouse. Emerick eased off the gas and hopped out of the driver's seat.

"Nick, wait here while I check."

"You are out of your mind," Chad said.

"My kid could be in there. I need to know."

He made his way out and ran at a crouch towards the bus, raking his rifle from side to side. The eighteen-wheeler was still jammed into the side of it, the door open and no one in the driver's side. He climbed up onto the bus and peered through the windows. There were bodies inside; many were kids, and soldiers lying unconscious. If the collision hadn't killed them, smoke inhalation might have, as it was filled inside with smoke making it hard to see anything except those that were closest to the windows. Shit, he thought, as he knew that the only way he would know was to climb inside.

Behind him he heard boots. Emerick turned, rifle on the ready, only to find Chad.

"You need some help?"

Chad pulled off his jacket and shirt, and tore off a portion of the shirt to wrap around his mouth and nostrils. "I'm going in. Keep watch," Chad said.

"You really are crazy."

"Hey, I wasn't the one that opted to go down into a nest of maniacs," Emerick said before climbing down through an area where a window had been shattered. He dropped and looked at the faces of the dead. His heart pounded in his chest at the thought of finding Devan. He didn't stay in there long, the air was thick and smoke so heavy that even with his face covered he could still smell plastic burning. He began coughing and heard Chad tell him to hurry up. He was going as fast as he could, walking on shattered glass and pulling at kids to see if it was his son. As he got to the far end of the bus, which was inside the church, he could see that some had managed to escape and were dead in the church itself.

"Devan!" he yelled but got no response. He climbed out where the front windshield once was. Someone had kicked it out, as it was lying crumpled off to one side. The bodies of several soldiers lay nearby. He stopped to collect a couple of handguns and some extra ammo before walking down the aisle of the church. Many of the pews had been reduced to rubble and fire had already left half of the building in a charred mess. "Devan?" He cried out his name again, anguish getting the better of him. A few tears formed at the corner of his eyes. That kid was everything to him. The only reason he got up each day. If he lost him he wasn't sure he'd be able to come back from that.

Satisfied that no one was there, he was about to head back when he heard gunfire outside. It wasn't just a single shot but multiple, and in rapid succession. He ran back to the bus and squeezed in and hauled himself back up the way he came until he could breathe fresh air again. That's when he saw what was happening. A group of armed individuals in Jeeps had swerved nearby and were taking cover and shooting at Chad who was now positioned behind the bus.

Emerick ducked and slid over the edge to join him.

He stayed low as bullets whizzed overhead.

It sound like hailstones as rounds ricocheted off metal, and lanced through windows.

"Where the hell did they come from?"

"Fuck knows. One second I'm peering into the bus, the next taking cover from these idiots."

"Infected?"

"No idea. Unless the infected have control of their

faculties enough to shoot rifles." Emerick cast a glance off towards the bus and noticed that Nick had got behind the wheel. The sound of hissing could be heard, followed by the sight of exhaust fumes rising as Nick pulled forward to provide additional cover using the bus. He swerved in close, and the doors opened. Jasper waved them in. Chad moved first, taking a few strides and hopping up inside, followed by Emerick. Everyone took cover as bullets peppered windows and metal, turning the whole damn thing into Swiss cheese. Whoever these lunatics were, they weren't messing around.

"Put your foot on it!" Chad yelled at Nick. He slammed his foot down and the bus reversed nearly taking out a building across the street. Emerick saw the men jump into their Jeeps and he knew they weren't going to give up. What they wanted was anyone's guess. Had they been the ones responsible for the eighteen-wheeler smashing the school bus? Was this some kind of local gang or militia? Armed, unregulated militia groups were a big thing in Texas. There were several. He'd had a couple of the leaders on his radio station over the years. They weren't extremists, just everyday folks passionate about their country and state. But in the eyes of the government they were a wild card, a possible threat that would stand against them if push came to shove. In recent months, warnings had already been issued to military commanders because of the conflict that was stirred as immigrants had tried to cross the border from Mexico to the USA and militia had shown up. Was this what was happening here? Emerick looked at Chad. Perhaps it wasn't them they were after but Chad.

"Nick, get out of the seat."

"What?"

Emerick grabbed him by the collar and yanked him out. He slipped behind the wheel, jammed it into drive and crushed the accelerator forcing the bus towards the Jeeps before they had time to follow. He saw the looks on their faces as the bus came barreling towards them. Several of them dived out of their vehicles seconds before he drove straight into the Jeeps. The crunch of metal, and the smash of glass echoed as he tore through the three Jeeps like a hot knife through butter and kept going down Lincoln until he saw a second yellow bus. This one was parked near the Palace Theater.

Was he in there?

"Hold on tight," Emerick said as he yanked the steering wheel. They went over the lawn and he brought it close to the main entrance. Knowing the area, and the best place to get a view of the theater and any threats, he killed the engine off and hopped out.

"GO! Everyone out."

They had seconds before the group they'd plowed through caught up with them.

Chad fired a few rounds at the door where a thick lock and chain had been looped around the handles to prevent anyone from entering. The chain slipped away and they entered and looked for anything they could use to barricade the door temporarily.

"Jasper, Nick, pile up those chairs over here." Emerick pulled off his belt and tied it around the handles of the door to secure it. He used the chain from the outside as a secondary measure and then began helping to pile up chairs, tables, anything to block the door and make it just a little harder for them to get in. He was familiar with the Second Empire style courthouse. Having visited many times over the years, it was a central point of interest and a historical landmark. Folks came from miles around to see it. It had four entrances, one on either of its four sides, and a tall tower with a central dome that overlooked the city. As soon as they had the first entrance blocked they moved on to the next, working furiously to barricade themselves in. From there they would head up to the tower inside the dome to get a better scope of the situation. Right now the streets were too hot to be out there.

* * *

The steady sound of gunfire echoed loudly outside and inside the Palace Theater. Devan huddled among the other students who had been told to stay low and together. He had lost track of how long they'd been in there. Four soldiers watched over them while the other eight had spread out to deal with the threat. All of them looked scared. This wasn't the Middle East, and those weren't insurgents outside. Whatever was causing this went far beyond that.

After being caught back at the school and thrown into the gymnasium like a second-class citizen he'd heard a couple of the soldiers talking about a pandemic, and heading off to a FEMA camp.

That might have worked had they managed to keep control of the situation but things had spiraled out of control when several students went batshit crazy, and parents showed up at the school. Rounds fired, and chaos ensued. If a soldier hadn't guided him out he was sure he would have been among the dead.

While he didn't like the situation, there was a certain level of comfort he drew from knowing that the military was trying to protect them, at least that's what he thought. He'd heard rounds go off in the school and many students didn't join them on the bus.

What happened? That was anyone's guess.

Still, they made it two blocks before the yellow bus ahead of them was T-boned by an eighteen-wheeler and they came under attack from what one of the soldiers said was a local militia.

Militia, the infected, it was all the same to him — a crazy bunch of lunatics trying to kill.

He stared down at old chewing gum on the ground. The place stank of mothballs and stale popcorn. For years the Art Deco style theater had operated as an opera house until it was turned into a movie theater that eventually closed in the 1970s. He'd heard all manner of rumors circulating about the place. There were plans to reopen it, someone else said they were going to turn it into a coffeehouse, and another said the city was going to knock it down. He'd always wondered what it looked like inside and had hoped they'd one day open it for the public to browse. He just never imagined he would see it under these conditions.

It wasn't those outside getting in that worried him

most, it was the soldiers.

He'd already overhead two of them talking about cleaning up shop. He didn't need to know military lingo to understand what that meant. If it came down to it, Uncle Sam would have no qualms about cutting ties.

All he could do was hope his father would get him out of this mess. He sighed and glanced at his phone. The battery was dead. If his father didn't reach him soon, he would be too.

Chapter 22

It was agreed. Gottman and Michael would go with Brody to Marfa, the rest would stay. Liam said he would watch over Jenna and make sure nothing happened. His only concern was with Sorenson. Although he'd made it clear that he had no allegiance to the government, his role in dealing with the infected and finding a cure made him a valuable asset. The question was whether or not the military would search for him. Gottman acted all nonchalant about it. "She'll be fine, Brody. Come on, we need to get moving before daylight. The only thing we have working for us right now is the darkness."

He led them down the hallway of his house, and through a door into the garage. As there was no power, he fumbled around in the dark then switched on a flashlight. A large white beam illuminated the inside of his two-car garage. On one side was a Jeep Wrangler and the other was covered up with a tarp. Michael jogged over to the

Wrangler and was about to hop in when Gottman said, "Nah, hold up. We'll take Lexi."

"Lexi?" Brody asked, a frown wrinkled his forehead.

"Ah, you haven't seen the new addition to my collection."

"Collection?"

"Yeah, I'm thinking of building it over time. By the time I hit retirement I aim to have six vehicles." He wandered around to the back of the hidden vehicle and took a large clump of the tarp. "Guys. Let me introduce you to Lexi. Or as I like to say, Sexy Lexi."

Brody raised an eyebrow, as did Michael. Gottman yanked hard on the tarp, pulling it away to reveal a brand-new Ford Mustang, blue with a white stripe. "Holy cow!" Michael said. "That's a sexy beast."

"Isn't she?" He ran his fingers over the top. "It's a 2018 Ford Mustang GT500. The cream of the crop. I had to have one. Been vying for one of these since I was kid." He pressed a button on a key fob and told them to hop in.

"You sure you want to take this?"

"We need to get in and out fast. You're damn right I do."

Brody shrugged and got in the passenger side while Michael slipped into the back. It smelled like a brand-new car. Clean. Zero dust. The thing was spotless inside.

Gottman opened the garage manually, then ran over to the house door and asked for someone to shut it after they left. Next he hopped in and fired up the engine. "Doesn't that just purr like a kitten?" He grinned like a madman and revved the engine a few times before rolling slowly out into the night. Michael leaned forward from the back with his arms wrapped around the front seats.

"Just curious but how do you intend to get out of Alpine if there are checkpoints and the town is surrounded by soldiers?"

"I'm pretty sure a Humvee can't outrun a Mustang," Gottman said slamming his foot against the accelerator and forcing Michael back against his seat. He took off at a high rate of speed zipping down the streets like he was driving a police cruiser with the lights on.

"Gottman," Brody said. "He has a point. You might be able to outrun them but that's if you can get by them."

"Obviously neither of you fine folks have seen *Smokey and the Bandit*."

Brody palmed his forehead. He was beginning to understand why they gave him the job of chief instead of Gottman. The Mustang powered down West Avenue, then hung a right down South Halbert Street before taking a right onto the Hogan Loop.

"As soon as you hit I-90 they are going to stop you. The checkpoint is just past Big Bend Brewing Company."

"Who said we are taking I-90?" Gottman replied without even looking at him. He had this wild grin on his face like a five-year-old kid reenacting some racecar driver fantasy. Brody had put his seat belt on and shot Michael a glance to make it clear that if he were smart he would do the same. There was no telling what Gottman had in mind but it seemed like it was going to be one hell of a bumpy ride.

Sure enough, he never hung a right to go north up to I-90, instead he powered off the road and tore through a farmer's field, knocking down tall brown grass. It battered the front of his car as they screamed across the field and he looked to his right to stay parallel to the road, using it as a means of establishing where he was heading. He kept his lights off and remained a good distance from the road to ensure the military blockade wouldn't see or hear them. "I told you. These guys are amateurs. They can't be watching the town twenty-four seven. If we've got out, you can be damn sure others have," Gottman said.

Brody thought of the implications of those in the town escaping. On one hand it would be good for anyone not infected but if the infected got out...he didn't want to imagine how quickly this could spread. It had been seventy-two hours since the El Paso Zoo event.

His mind switched back to the present moment. Out of the corner of his eye, two luminescent yellow eyes cut through the night, getting larger by the second.

"Uh, Gottman."

"Yeah?"

"Looks like we got company."

He turned to see a military Jeep in hot pursuit.

* * *

Gottman had entertained the thought of a high-speed chase since he was a kid, in fact it was the very reason he became a cop. What other job gave them the right to put the pedal to the metal and break the speed limit? He'd considered a career as a racecar driver but where was the fun in that? Being a cop combined his love of weapons, law and vehicles all into one. Yet he'd only been involved in a few high-speed chases. His superior who put public safety as number one had called off most of them. That's what most of the public didn't know. There were rules that applied to them as cops. They had to abide by them and sometimes that meant calling off a chase, and letting the next town over handle it. It pissed him off to no end but not tonight. This was a free-for-all.

Still, he wasn't going to jeopardize his baby.

This car was in mint condition. Sure, he didn't mind

getting it dirty but if that Jeep got any closer, he was pretty sure they would open fire and the thought of his expensive vehicle being turned into a metal strainer wasn't good.

Instead, he swerved the vehicle, slammed it into park and got out.

"Gottman. What are you doing?"

He didn't respond. He went to the trunk as calm as could be and popped it open. He pulled out an M107 Barrett .50 caliber rifle. The damn thing was a monster, and the best part was that the gun laws treated it like any other hunting rifle, except this wasn't any other rifle. It could hit targets at more than 2,000 yards and inflict some serious damage. He brought it around and slapped a magazine into it as he laid it on top of the car and climbed up to get into a better position. Once ready with his finger hovering over the trigger, he peered through the scope, watching the Jeep get closer.

"Gottman."

"Trust me, chief."

He heard him mumble and curse as Gottman took a deep breath and lined up the target. Under his breath he whispered, "That's it. Come on. You picked the wrong fucking night to be a hero. Let's hope they paid you enough." He pressed the soft part of his finger against the trigger and gave them a few more seconds before he unloaded a round directly into the front of the engine. He quickly set up the next shot, this time aiming lower for the wheel. "Don't fail me now, baby!" Another ear-piercing shot rang out and the military-grade vehicle looked like it buckled, and the driver lost control. In the next instant it twisted and flipped, catapulting out the occupants, and rolled once, then twice before coming to rest.

"Oorah, jarheads!"

He quickly slipped off the vehicle and tossed the rifle into the rear and hopped back in the driver's side as though he'd just returned from taking a pee break. "They should have joined the police force." Brody glanced at him with a slack jaw as he tore out of there sending a wave of loose mud into the air.

"You can thank me later," Gottman said with a smile on his face.

* * *

"You want to tell me how the hell this happened?" the president asked, an expression of anger on his face. It was okay for him to act like God from the Oval Office but he wasn't the one in the field, it wasn't his boots on the ground. Lynch sat in front of her computer with the president in a square on the left and Margaret Wells from FEMA on the right. Lynch had been trying to explain how she'd lost contact with Major Tim Brown and the platoons in both towns. Behind her waiting to step in if need be was Mosley. Unknown to the president but having made a name for himself, he would be her lifeline if this all went south — a final attempt to convince him that she had this in hand. The fact was she didn't. There had been no contact with the major since she last spoke to him. By any measure she was treating him as a casualty of war. For that's what this outbreak had become now. All there was left to do was clean up and hope to God they'd managed to contain this to the state of Texas.

Tired of listening to Lynch's excuses, he turned his anger towards the FEMA rep. "Margaret, please tell me you have some good news?"

She gritted her teeth together and her lips pulled back — an expression of discomfort not much different than Lynch. Clearly the answer was no. She took a glass of water and sipped some before setting it to one side and trying to compose herself. It wouldn't matter how she tried to word it, unless she was delivering good news he wouldn't take it well.

"Unfortunately I have bad news. It's spreading."

"Why am I not surprised," he replied.

She felt a little bit better. At least she wouldn't bear the brunt of all his anger. Not that she really cared. At this point the chances of recovering from this if it had spread further afield were slim to none. What could they do? Soldiers had been sent into two small towns and not even they could contain it. Killing people wasn't the solution.

Without tests they would be ending the lives of innocent people. It could be an act of genocide unlike anything seen before.

No, this had to be stopped using medical means.

Sorenson. Her mind went to him and she made a mental note to contact him as soon as she got off the call. In all the drama of losing contact with the military, she'd completely forgot about his work at the hospital. A quick call and maybe, hopefully, he could establish what could be done, if anything. They still had people who were immune. That was something.

"Sir, we have been in contact with hospitals throughout the state of Texas. There have been numerous symptoms cropping up in six locations. We have had our teams head there and contain what we can but we can't be sure that it hasn't spread beyond the hospitals."

"So what is the solution? Do you even have one?"

"The immunes," Lynch chimed in, hoping to be some light in the darkest hour.

"And what of these immunes? Where are they? Have

you tested them to be sure they can help others?"

"No. We just know that six of them are immune. Dr. Daniel Sorenson is working with them to determine if their blood might hold the key to at least preventing escalation of the disease or virus, whatever you want to call it."

"I want to call it a fuck-up. Can I?" the president said in a frank manner.

"Call it what you will. If this has spread throughout Texas we are going to need a vaccine, and right now the only solution we have is to be found in those individuals."

"Who are where?"

"In Alpine. At the hospital."

"The same one that was overrun."

She felt her stomach sink before she nodded. "Yes. The same one."

"So there is a possibility they are dead?"

She wasn't going to lie. What was the point? If this was the house of cards falling in on itself, was she responsible for ensuring the survival of the nation or did it rest in the hands of their commander in chief?

"So what are we looking at, Margaret? A couple of hospitals?"

She shook her head. "I'm going to play you some footage of Dallas and Houston."

This was new to even Lynch. Her head had been so buried in the work at the towns that she hadn't even considered what was occurring beyond that. A stream of video came into view of people attacking each other on the streets, followed by police trying to intervene with smoke grenades. It looked like a riot but it wasn't a group protesting, or even a violent rally, it was ordinary people trying to kill each other. Many were fleeing and screaming as if fear itself was chasing them down or as if patients from a mental ward had gotten loose in the city.

"They are doing everything they can to stop it but..."

The president closed his eyes and then squeezed the bridge of his nose as he sat back in his leather seat. "Sir, might I suggest implementing a code red?" Lynch said.

His eyes snapped open. He knew what that meant.

"You're telling me it's got that out of hand that you see no other alternative?"

"May I speak?" Mosley said stepping into view behind Lynch. She wanted to prevent him but as they hadn't come up with any better solutions perhaps he could see the solution from the outside looking in.

"You are?" the president asked.

"Lieutenant Mosley, sir."

Lynch piped up. "He's been involved in numerous black ops projects that could have easily spiraled out of control."

"I would like to take in a few Chinooks and pull our men out then implement a code red. Right now our military is the most valuable asset we have and if this has slipped out of our grasp then their energy would be better served in the larger cities, like Dallas and Houston."

"And what of these small towns?"

Mosley cocked his head. He didn't need to say. The president understood. It wasn't like he hadn't heard a suggestion like what Mosley had in mind. "Right now, sir, all we can do is prevent this from becoming a larger threat. We deal with the towns as a whole and then use our soldiers to wipe out those remaining. If we leave them in there they don't stand a chance. They will be overrun if they haven't already. It's a method to the madness."

"Madness. You've got that right. How long do you need?"

"Two, maybe three hours tops. We'll pull out as many as we can and then have the Air Force handle the rest. We'll reassess after the aftermath and roll in to address any further threats. I can't imagine there would be many."

The president nodded and looked away from the camera. Lynch could tell he was contemplating it. All they needed was the go-ahead. "I will need to speak with the Joint Chiefs before we go code red but in the meantime, you have my approval to send in Chinooks. And lieutenant, get in and get out fast. I would hate to see you join the major."

With that said he hung up and his screen went black. Margaret asked if there were any questions Lynch had before exiting herself. Lynch closed her laptop and rose, spreading her fingers on the table and nodding slowly, taking in everything that he'd said and agreeing that it was the best course of action.

"Ma'am?"

"Yes, Mosley."

"We got this. You have my word, if the major is in there, we will find him."

"Of course you will because I'm coming with you."

"But, I thought…"

"I've worked with Major Brown for a long time and I know he would do the same for me." She walked past him without saying another word, and then heard him follow.

Chapter 23

The onslaught of heavy gunfire was steady. Not all of it was targeting the Presidio County Courthouse. Nick turned to Chad whose back was against the wall in the interior of the central rotunda. Every few seconds he would take a sneak peek around the corner and then back the other way. Emerick was on the other side watching the east and south, while Chad covered the west and north entranceways. The slightest movement of the doors and they would unleash a torrent of rounds to ward off those looking to break in. Nick was meant to assist where and when needed. Emerick still didn't think he was capable of doing much more than get in the way even though if it wasn't for him — well, for Jasper — they wouldn't have even made it out of the school grounds.

"You know what, I'm heading up. Try to get a bird's-eye view of what's happening."

"Careful," Emerick said

"I'll stay out of the way."

"No, I meant don't shoot yourself, or Jasper for that matter," Emerick said before chuckling. Nick scowled and flipped him the bird before dashing out into the fatal funnel and across to the stairs that would take them up three floors before giving them access to the central dome — a room with windows wrapped 360 degrees. He'd been there years ago on a school trip. It was probably the highlight of the entire day. He and Devan and sat up there having a smoke with one of the windows open while the rest of the goofballs followed Ms. Mendes around on a guided tour. By the time they rejoined the class, they'd wasted thirty minutes and she was none the wiser. As much as Emerick was worried about his son, so was Nick. Devan was the only real friend he had. Of course he knew people in the school but only to give a nod to, or make a passing comment in class. Devan had been with him through thick and thin. They'd bonded over their commonality of their parents fighting, and the eventual separation, and of course their love of rock music, and all things guitar.

Jasper followed in his shadow like a lost puppy. "Are we going to die?"

"Well you aced math, what do you think?" Nick said. He was clearing the floors as he went. The thought of one of those crazed lunatics coming after him remained at the forefront of his mind as they made their way up.

"Well um, the probability based on the current situation is pretty high."

Nick looked back at him over his shoulder before they took to the steps that led up to the dome. "Jasper, you heard from your father since this kicked off?"

"No, he's out of town."

"So you're staying with your mother."

"No. It's just me."

Nick glanced at him.

"Well where's your mother?"

"She passed away when I was six. Breast cancer."

"Ah man, that sucks. Sorry to hear that."

"Ah it's okay. I was too young to really grasp it. You

don't miss what you've never really had, right?"

"I guess," Nick said as they arrived in the dome and looked out across Marfa. At night they should have been able to see lights all across the town. It should have been lit up like a damn Christmas tree but the only light came from fires burning in the town, and the odd flashlight that clicked on and off. "Hey, uh, keep down." Jasper crouched and made his way over to one of the windows and peered out. Nick also peered out trying to get a better scope of what was going on. He could see the silhouettes of figures darting across the courthouse yard, and the muzzle flash of guns on top of the Palace Theater. Under the light of the moon he could make out the second yellow school bus. "Jasper, how many buses did they take out?"

"Two."

"All right. So he's got to be on that one. And if those muzzle flashes on the Palace Theater are anything to go by, there's a chance he's in there." He was planning on telling Emerick but he knew that he would do something stupid and right now they were protected. More gunshots erupted from downstairs. If they could keep them distracted he could exit via one of these windows, slip down onto the roof and make his way down one of the drainpipes at the side of the building. It was a long way down. Three stories but it could be done. Those assholes who were attempting to get in wouldn't be expecting it. Would they? Maybe all of them could go out that way? His mind was beginning to run away on him, a series of crisscrossing ideas from the logical to the absurd.

"Let's head down."

They had only taken a few steps when they heard a loud crash down below, and the building itself shook. Nick braced himself against the wall then hurried down at the sound of gunfire. He'd only made it down two stories when he was met by Emerick and Chad coming the other way. "Go. Go. GO! They've breached the building."

"How?" Nick yelled as he and Jasper turned back the way they came.

"Drove the damn bus through the doorway."

It looked like they had no choice. When they reached the small dome room, Nick pushed open one of the windows and began to climb out. Emerick grabbed him by the arm. "Are you out of your mind? You know how high we are?"

"You want to go down. Be my guest."

"He has a point," Chad said climbing out after him. Jasper was next followed by Emerick who hesitated but after hearing more gunfire down below followed suit. The courthouse had a series of gray sloped roofs on top of pink stucco brick. One slip and it would be over. A hard wind blew against them as Emerick closed the window behind him and balanced on the edge before jumping down and joining the others.

"How the hell did I end up in this mess?" Emerick asked. "On day I'm on the radio, the next on the damn Presidio County Courthouse roof."

They carefully but quickly located the gutter and the nearest metal drainpipe and one by one they scaled down the side.

* * *

Sergio had begun to see double. They'd left the veterinarian's with the hopes of getting out of town but since having that needle jabbed in his leg he'd been feeling nauseated, and barely able to keep his eyes open.

"You okay, buddy?" Lars asked, his voice deepening, as his face divided into three. It was like being inside a fun house. Every movement he made was exaggerated as though he'd drunk his way through a case of beer.

"I'm not feeling well," he said bending at the waist thinking he was about to throw up. He supported himself against the wall of the vet's and breathed heavily.

"You want to take a minute?" Lars asked.

He shook his head. "No, we need to keep moving."

"What about the dog?"

"Just leave the door open. Let him go."

He might have taken the dog had his mind not felt so foggy, but he was having trouble standing, hearing, seeing, even breathing. "S...er...gio!" Lars said, his voice stretched out. Sergio shook his head again and staggered over to the dirt bike He grasped the handlebars and tried to get on but lost his balance and tipped the whole bike over. Crashing on top he heard Lars come up behind him as he slipped in and out of consciousness.

"Sergio."

His name was the last thing he heard.

* * *

When he came to, he woke up to a rough tongue licking his face.

He swatted at the blurry face above him before the world snapped into view. It was the dog. He was lying on a carpet and staring up at a fan. A light flickered off to the right of him. Sergio turned his head and his gaze became transfixed on a candle before he saw Lars hobble into the room. "Where are we?" he asked.

"Finally, you're awake."

"How long have I been out?"

"An hour. I thought you were a goner. You gave me a scare back there. I went back inside and took a look at that syringe. It's some kind of anesthetic. Probably wasn't enough to knock you out completely but she gave you one hell of a dose. Enough to put a dog down for twenty-four hours, that's for sure. I'm thinking your dog over here got lucky."

"It isn't my dog." He sat up and rubbed his forearm across his face to wipe away drool that had trickled out of his mouth.

"Well he sure has taken a liking to you."

He looked around. "How did we get here?"

"Ah, well we have Arthur to thank for that."

"Who?"

"Me," a raspy voice said before he began coughing.

Sergio turned to see an old-timer sitting in a recliner chair, with a beer in hand. He had white wispy hair that looked as if it hadn't seen a pair of scissors in the last decade. He was wearing a plaid shirt, and a worn pair of jeans. His skin was a pasty white and judging from the large basket of tissues near his armchair, and the hacking cough, he was either a smoker or Lars had just accepted help from someone who was infected. Sergio backed up a little and both of them stared.

"Who have you been around?" Sergio asked as he patted down his own body looking for his handgun.

Lars noticed and handed it over. "I have it."

As soon as he got a grip on it, he pointed it at the old man. "I asked, who have you been around!"

Lars frowned and got between them. "Steady, Sergio. Are you out of your goddamn mind? Arthur here helped us."

"He's sick."

"You got that right," he said coughing again.

Sergio's nostrils flared and he aimed the gun and Lars put his hands up. "Hold on a minute. He's on a respirator for smoking. COPD. Back off. He's not like the others."

"No? And you just bought his word on that?"

"Sergio, put the gun down."

Arthur reached for a pack of smokes. "If you're going to squeeze the trigger, son, squeeze it, otherwise I'll have a smoke. Doctor says I shouldn't but I don't have long so I don't think it matters now." He started coughing hard again before tapping one out and lighting it. Slowly, Sergio lowered the gun but kept his gaze on him.

"Okay. Okay. That's good. Here, have a beer," Lars turned and reached for a can and tossed him one. "The dog. The one you called Baxter. He's actually called Sonny. It's his."

"When the lights went out, and all that rioting on the streets started, I figured I would go get my dog. He was meant to go in and get a chip put in and it should have been a quick operation, like two minutes but the vets screwed up the scheduling and had some other operation booked for that day. So I left him there with plans on picking him up that evening." He took a hard pull on his cigarette. "Like I said, when all this shit happened…" He started coughing and reached for some tissues, then spat into one and rolled it and tossed it in the can beside him. It toppled over the edge onto the carpet which was caked in them. "I couldn't get out. So I had to wait until the middle of the night, and that's when I came across you two asshats."

"Asshats?"

The old timer chuckled.

"Well seriously? You take your friend to a vet for a bullet wound?"

"There was nowhere else to take him. The hospital's quarantined."

He shrugged and took another hard pull on his cigarette. "Anyway, you can stay here the night if you like. Looks like your pal could use some rest and well, you don't look well yourself."

"Don't push me, old man."

He chuckled. "What, you going to kill me? You'd be doing me a favor, son. Which reminds me. I've been looking for someone to take Sonny here. He seems to have taken a liking to you. You want to take him?"

"He's your dog, grandpa."

The old man snorted. "I can't get out like I used to."

"Do I look like a fucking dog sitter?" Sergio said.

"Sergio," Lars chimed in shaking his head.

Sergio glanced at the dog then back at Arthur. "You

look as if you could live a few more years. I'm sure the dog would prefer to stay with you."

"Look outside, son, this ain't no place for an old man and a dog."

Sergio got up and stumbled into the wall. "Whoa!" Lars came to his aid and he swatted him off. "I'm fine." He glanced out the window and that's when he saw what Arthur was talking about. His apartment was located downtown overlooking the main drag. The town was ablaze. Stores, homes, vehicles. There were people attacking one another, hurting themselves and fleeing. "Holy shit."

Chapter 24

Sorenson got off the phone with clear instructions. He didn't need to be reminded, he understood the gravity of the situation and the many lives across the nation that were at risk. He let out a large sigh and looked at the group in the kitchen talking — Jenna was upstairs. He wasn't a violent man by nature but he was prepared to do whatever it took for the survival of his country. If that meant holding them captive, so be it. For that's what it all boiled down to. The only thing was he didn't know his location. Without the location he couldn't call Lynch back to arrange extraction of the immunes.

Of course he couldn't just come out with it. He could already sense their apprehension with him after all they'd been put through at the hospital. They'd treated them like lab rats, overriding their civil rights and ignoring their protests.

He wandered down the hall towards the front door to

check the side table for mail. There had to be something with an address on it — a letter, flyer or newspaper.

"Everything okay, Sorenson?" Liam asked, stepping out into the hallway as Sorenson pulled out a drawer from a small table. He turned and with a nervous tone to his voice tried to act normal.

"Yeah. Fine."

"Who was that you were speaking with?"

"Just my wife. Back in Chicago. Wanted to make sure she was okay."

"Huh," Liam said nodding slowly. "Strange that you managed to get a signal," he said taking out his phone and holding it up. "As none of us can get anything."

"Satellite. A satellite phone. Yeah, issued by the CDC. Kind of handy really. Quite often they send us to remote areas that don't have good coverage and we need to stay in contact with them and loved ones."

Liam slowly walked towards him, tucking his own phone back into his pocket. He'd been given a handgun by Officer Gottman and told to watch over the group while the officers were away. If anyone attempted to break in, he was to take care of business. Whether or not he could do it was to be seen. The way he'd acted at the hospital hadn't exactly instilled confidence in Sorenson. It was because of that he had contemplated whether or not he could take him if push came to shove.

"Any movement outside?" Liam asked.

So far they'd been lucky. The street outside was quiet, except for the odd pop of gunfire in the distance. From what he'd been able to gauge, they were in a small suburban neighborhood, a cul-de-sac, but it was too dark to make out the street sign. Sorenson shook his head.

"What are you searching for?"

"Just curious as to where we are."

"Alpine."

"Right. I know that. I'm talking about the street."

"Why? They said they would return." Liam got closer. Sorenson closed the drawer and turned to face him. Liam was still wearing his white lab coat. He was around six foot one, and skinny.

Feeling pushed into a corner, Sorenson came up with an excuse. "Just in case we die here, I want my wife to know where my body is."

Liam's eyebrow went up. "Yeah, well you don't have to worry about that. As long as we stay put, stay quiet and wait, I'm sure we'll be fine."

Sorenson nodded. "Any alcohol?"

Liam looked at him skeptically. "I came across a bottle of bourbon in the living area," he said jerking his chin over his shoulder but maintaining narrow eye contact. Sorenson could tell he didn't trust him. None of them did. Gottman had told Liam to keep a close eye on him while they were gone. He expected that was what made this even more difficult. The last thing he wanted to do was find himself wrestling for that weapon. He'd always used communication as a tool for deescalating situations and in his mind this was no different.

"Let's get a drink, shall we?" Sorenson suggested. Liam nodded and they headed into the living area. It was a typical bachelor pad with black leather couches, a throw rug, a coffee table at the center, and a small makeshift bar in the corner of the room. Sorenson glanced at the 50-inch TV on the wall while Liam went around to the bar and set the gun on the counter. He pulled out two glasses and poured two fingers of amber. Leaving the gun in place he made his way around and handed him one before returning and collecting the gun. Sorenson berated himself inwardly. He should have gone for it while it was on the counter. No, stick to the plan. Get him relaxed and eventually someone would tell him where they were. He took a hard swig on his drink almost downing it in one gulp. It burned as it slipped down his throat.

"Ah, now that's what I needed. Just a little something to take the edge off."

Liam pursed his lips and nodded scanning the room. "So you think there is hope for us?"

"Of course. I mean, it's a bad situation but we've seen worse."

"You have?"

"Not in this country but elsewhere."

"I guess the government kept that hushed, right?" Liam downed his drink and returned to fill his glass. He set the gun down for a second time, this time turning his back.

"They do what needs to be done to protect the many."

"Yeah, and is killing innocents included in that?"

Sorenson saw his opportunity. He knew this wasn't going to get any easier. Liam would be watching him like a hawk. Now if he could get his hands on that Glock he might be able to speed up this process. Time was working against them. Three hours and the military would be wiping this town off the map. He intended to be far, far away by then. Sorenson grabbed a fire poker and held it behind him and approached. Liam twisted and Sorenson reacted fast to deflect attention. He extended his glass. "Mind filling that again?"

"Sure."

He turned and Sorenson took advantage of the moment. He lashed out, scything the air with the metal poker and striking Liam across the back of the head. He let out a groan and fell forward. Sorenson expected him to drop but he didn't. Liam's hand darted to the gun and latched on to it. *No, no,* Sorenson thought as he lunged forward and slammed into him pressing him up against the bar so he couldn't turn. He grasped his wrist and they wrestled for control. At some point Liam pushed himself back and they toppled over the couch and crashed into the table. The sound of boots could be heard approaching as they continued to fight. Before anyone could intervene, the gun went off. A loud crack, and then all resistance dissipated. Sorenson pulled back and stared at Liam's shirt as blood soaked it. A gasp was heard. He looked up to see the group staring at him. His hand was still on the gun, though shaking now. Liam gasped for air, and then clutched the wound, words trying to escape his mouth. Nothing formed except a few final breaths.

"What have you done?" Gina the pharmacist asked. "What have you done!" she screamed. Sorenson reacted fast by raising the gun and telling them to stay back. The sound of feet coming down the stairs could be heard, and then Jenna emerged pushing her way through the group to see what all the commotion was. She glanced down then at Sorenson.

"I didn't want it to go like this but he gave me no other option."

He reached into his pocket for his phone and tapped in a number. "Now you're going to tell me the number and street we are on, or..." he trailed off as the phone connected with Colonel Lynch.

* * *

Five minutes earlier one of three Chinooks had landed carrying Mosley's crew of soldiers, a small elite team of special operatives trained to deal with the worst. Using a beacon from the helicopter Major Brown was on, they were able to pinpoint the exact location of his last known whereabouts.

Colonel Lynch stood looking at the charred wreckage of the helicopter, and the bodies of the fallen. Among them was Major Brown. He'd been stripped of his military fatigues and had multiple stab wounds. The men around him were shot, hacked to death or strangled. It was a brutal sight and one that would stay with her forever. No one deserved to go out that way. Lynch thought of Brown's family. His young daughters that would never have their father walk them down the aisle or get to hold him again.

The phone in her pocket rang. She let it go to voice, distracted by her thoughts. Mosley and the team of six spread out ensuring her safety. The phone jangled again and this time she answered it. The caller ID was Sorenson.

"Go ahead."

"43 Turner Avenue."

"Roger that," the colonel said still lost in her thoughts. "We'll be there shortly. Make sure you're ready to go."

Sorenson cleared his throat. "Colonel, we are short one. He attacked. I had no other choice."

Lynch nodded. "Doesn't matter, all we need is one of them."

She hung up and updated Mosley. "We leave in five.

Gather up the bodies in the other Chinooks. Fly them back to the FEMA camp. Their families will want to know what happened. They died as heroes."

Mosley showed no emotion. He was used to seeing such horrors. Lynch wasn't. Sure, she had seen her share of war but not like this. This was vindictive. She turned her head at the sound of gunfire nearby. They needed to move fast. This wasn't the only soldier that needed assistance. One by one they loaded the dead into a Chinook and it took off leaving the other two. The steady thump of rotors sent waves of wind her way as she stayed low and made her way back to the helicopter. They boarded and took off, this time heading for Turner Avenue.

* * *

Sorenson had gathered them all in the kitchen and was keeping the handgun on them. Jenna leaned against the counter unable to believe it had come to this.

"You don't owe them anything. Why are you doing this?" she asked.

"This isn't about owing anyone. It's about the survival of our nation. When I chose to work for the CDC I signed up to protect, just as you signed up to help those in need. This is me helping. You've seen it yourselves. We are losing control of this situation. Give it another two or three days and this will extend beyond Texas. Dallas and Houston are already overwhelmed. Military are in the cities now trying to handle this through preventative measures."

"You mean killing people?" Gina said. She stood with her arms crossed and a scowl on her face. Beside her were Pete Douglas the security guard and Jenna.

"If this spreads any further it won't matter if we have a cure or not. Attempting to get it to those in need will be near impossible. You must understand the gravity of this situation. You are the last hope we have. I cannot allow anything to jeopardize that. Liam would have tried to stop me."

"I have kids," Gina said. "I need to see them."

"And you will but we need to take samples from you

all and use that to create a vaccine for this threat before it gets out of control."

The sound of gunshots echoed loudly, nearer than before. Jenna thought about Brody and Nick and wished she had gone with her husband.

"Where will they take us?" Jenna asked.

"Chicago. We have the tools, the equipment, labs and team to develop what's needed."

"How can you live with what you've done?" Pete asked.

"You'll thank me one day. Look, I get it. This is bad news. I know you don't understand what we are trying to do here and I don't expect you to, but if this works then you will one day look back at this and realize that what was done was for the benefit of the world, not just our nation but the world at large."

"You already took samples of our blood."

"Yes, back at the hospital, before the breach. We can't risk going back in there."

"Just extract what you need here and leave us," Jenna

said.

"While it's very possible what is needed may be in the blood, it could reside in another area, so we may have to take multiple samples of bone marrow, tissue and blood. We won't know until we can see how your bodies are managing to resist this—" he trailed off and Gina cut him off.

"This self-made plague."

He glanced at her and then back at Jenna before taking a few steps back and peering out the window.

"If they're arriving by chopper, I'd think you'd hear them," Pete said.

Out the corner of her eye, Jenna saw Gina reach back behind her and take hold of a large bread knife and extract it from its wooden housing. She wanted to cry out and stop her but she realized that if they didn't do something, all the effort Brody and Gottman had taken to break her out of the hospital would be for nothing. And of course there was the fact that what the CDC had planned for them might not end in a small amount of

tissue being taken but a large amount from the brain —
as that was the area that was damaged in the infected. If
she was going to die, it wasn't going to be in a lab. She
was more than willing to hand over her blood and a small
tissue sample but refused to be held captive and treated
like nothing more than a rat.

The second time Sorenson looked out the window,
Gina rushed forward, knife at waist height. Sorenson's
eyes flared, and he reacted, unloading two rounds just as
she drove the knife into him. It all happened so fast. Both
of them slumped onto the floor, Gina coughed and
spluttered and Sorenson tried to catch his breath.

Pete rushed forward and retrieved the gun from him
while Jenna checked on Gina.

It was too late. She was struggling to breathe.

Sorenson stared blankly as if realizing his fate was
sealed.

"Jenna. My kids. Would you…"

She inhaled sharply and then never took the next
breath. Her eyes glazed over and Jenna ran her hand over

her face to close the lids. She was so angry, not just with Sorenson but the government. How could they let this happen? All their attempts to meddle had unleashed something so deadly that it didn't just kill; it destroyed families, stealing loved ones away from each other. For what? An attempt to make soldiers feel no fear?

Pete placed a hand on her shoulder.

"Jenna, we need to go."

The sound of a chopper could be heard getting closer.

She nodded, looked at Sorenson who was still alive and shook her head in disgust before darting out into the night in a final attempt to avoid becoming guinea pigs in further experiments.

Chapter 25

Angela had been acting strange ever since being attacked by her landlord. Twenty minutes earlier, they'd been waiting in the idling Chevy for Emerick and Nick when the violence erupted. Although they didn't want to leave them behind they had no choice. It was either that or be overrun, and they'd already seen a couple get dragged from their car and beaten to death in the street.

It was insane.

Callie couldn't believe it was happening.

Not in her town. Not in her country.

Initially Angela had driven a few blocks away with the idea to swing back around when the crowd dispersed but it never did. It only increased in size. It was as if the entire town had come out to celebrate some event, except pockets of violence dominated.

It was too risky to stay on the streets so Angela had taken them to her apartment, a gorgeous block on the south side. It was upscale, at least for Marfa. Angela said she got in when the prices were low but they'd soared over the past five years. She was convinced that Emerick would make his way there after getting out of the school, but Callie wasn't so sure. She'd seen the knot of people heading for the doors of the school; they'd witnessed the extreme acts of brutality. Things weren't going to get better.

They'd spent the last few hours in her apartment huddled around a flashlight, eating canned beans and peaches, as there was no electricity. If it wasn't for the fact that it was summer the situation could have been a lot worse.

Everything had been calm and peaceful until her landlord knocked on the door.

Angela had got up and peered out the peephole. For a brief moment she had contemplated not opening but when he called out her name, she figured it was safe — it wasn't. That was clear from the moment the door opened.

The six-foot, approximately 260-pound man pushed his way inside acting all erratic. He kept pacing back and forth biting on his nails, except he must have been doing it for some time as he'd worn them down so much that they were bleeding.

"Gerald," Angela said, backing up and keeping a hand out. "What do you want?"

"I need the rent. I need..." He initially sounded logical but then he would spill out words that didn't make any sense, and every few seconds he would stop walking and just stare at the wall as if he was stoned. The second Angela touched his arm to try and break the trancelike state he would cower back, his hands shaking so hard that he looked as if he was having a seizure.

"I've already paid you this month. Remember, I came into the office and cut you a check."

That was when it happened. It was like a switch being turned on. One second he was acting like he was afraid and the next a sneer formed on his face and he lunged forward, his hands wrapping around Angela's throat. She stumbled back over the coffee table and they collapsed on the floor. Shocked, Callie looked on unsure of what to do. Frantically, Angela raked at his face with her nails trying to pry him off but it had little effect on him. Her choking sounds got worse the longer he held her down. Angela turned her face and gestured by flaring her eyes. Callie came to her senses and grabbed hold of Gerald by the collar and began yanking at him. It was useless, one quick swipe of his arm and he knocked the wind out of her. Now both of them were coughing and gasping for air. Determined to not let him kill her, she rose, bent over and clung to her stomach as she staggered over to the kitchen. On one of the burners was a pan that must have been used the night before, as there was grease in it. Callie grabbed it up and turned. A second of hesitation and she brought it down as hard as she could across Gerald's face. It knocked him loose and he rolled over. Angela gasped for air and crawled away trying to put as much distance as she could between Gerald and her.

While the crack to the head had worked to get him off,

it hadn't knocked him out, and had only angered him more. Angela was of no use as she was still trying to suck in air. There was no telling how damaged her throat was. Gerald tried to rise to his feet but Callie acted swiftly and cracked him again, this time around the back of the head. Then she followed through once, twice, four more times until he was no longer moving. She didn't know if he was dead but he was unconscious, that was for sure.

Callie hurried over to Angela and placed a hand on her back.

"Are you okay?"

She grunted, and nodded while still holding her neck. Callie looked back at Gerald, and saw a pool of blood beginning to form around his head. The very sight of it made her feel sick to her stomach. She raced to the bathroom and threw up.

When she reemerged, Angela snatched up the keys off the counter.

"We can't stay here." She looked down at him, tucked the keys into her pocket and then began to drag his limp body out of her apartment. Callie offered to help but she refused. If anyone was going to get blame for this, she was. Angela kept saying that she was indebted to Callie and apologized for opening the door.

"You don't need to apologize," Callie said as she watched Angela stuff Gerald into a closet off the hallway. It was filled with cleaning fluid, a vacuum and a machine for cleaning carpets. As soon as he was out of the way they hurried to the vehicle with the intention of heading over to Callie's home and checking on her parents.

That was six hours ago.

They never made it to the apartment. Instead, they found themselves driving in circles, stopping, hiding and doing everything they could to avoid crazed lunatics who had taken to the streets. All the while Angela was getting more peculiar by the hour. At first it was nothing more than a faraway look in her eyes, then she began mumbling incoherently, then she would slam on the brakes and just stare down the road as if frozen. But it was when her hands started to shake, and she snapped at any suggestions Callie had that she became really worried.

"Angela, maybe…"

"NO!" she bellowed not even looking at her.

Now as if defaulting in her mind back to her old routine, she headed east towards the radio station. She kept saying they needed to go on the air and warn people. People needed to be warned, she said three or four times. Any attempt by Callie to sway her from that resulted in an angry glare. Eventually, Callie remained quiet hoping that when they made it to the station she would go in and Callie would part ways with her. The only thing that mattered to her right then was returning home and making sure her parents were okay.

As they turned onto Highland Avenue and got closer to the station, Angela slammed the brakes on and stared at the building off in the distance. She revved the engine a few times and Callie looked at her out the corner of her eye.

"Angela."

No response.

Callie went for the door but it was locked.

"Angela, let me out."

Nothing. No reply.

"Angela."

The engine roared, and Callie grabbed her seat belt and snapped it on. In that instant, Angela hit the accelerator as hard as she could. The wheels spun, and let out a squeal as they surged forward. She glanced at Angela who wasn't strapped in. Within seconds, the vehicle swerved off the road across the sidewalk and slammed straight through the front windows of the radio station, plowing through tables and chairs until it hit the rear wall and catapulted Angela out of her seat through the windshield.

That was the last image she remembered before the world went black.

Chapter 26

His heart beat a mile a minute. Brody exited the school building, shocked by the aftermath of violence. The three of them had to kill four people just to discover that Nick wasn't among the dead. Upon arriving in Marfa, they'd checked his home, thinking that Nick would have gone there and let himself in. The place was empty. There wasn't even any sign that he'd been there. No food had been taken out of the cupboards. The windows hadn't been opened. And his neighbor hadn't heard anyone. The school was the obvious next stop in the search.

As they emerged from the school and returned to Gottman's vehicle, Brody tried to think where else he might have gone. The only name that came to mind was Devan, Emerick's son. They'd practically grown up together, attended the same school and were like two peas in a pod. Although since his separation from Jenna he'd fallen out of touch with Nick, he knew him well enough to know that wherever Devan was, Nick wouldn't be that far behind, especially in a situation like this.

They tore out of the lot, clipping a few lunatics in the process.

Gottman was outraged but it was unavoidable. The sheer number of people that had taken to the streets was overwhelming. They were either trying to escape the town or attack it. The GT screamed through the streets, a throaty rumble kicking out of the exhaust pipe as Gottman slalomed around abandoned vehicles and people who chose to stand in the street despite the GT barreling towards them.

"Move here, my girlfriend said. It's beautiful, she said. The people are real nice. Oh yeah, real nice, more like fifty shades of crazy!" Michael said leaning forward from the back seat.

As they came around onto Lincoln Street they could finally see what all the commotion was. It was like a war zone. Various individuals had positioned themselves behind burnt-out cars and were taking potshots at each other.

Gottman slammed the brakes on and squinted. "That's a school bus up ahead."

He glanced at Brody and didn't need to say anything, they were thinking the same. They were positioned about two blocks down from the white church where the school bus was embedded. Although they were out of range, they were far from out of trouble.

"I've got to see."

"Hey, I'm all for finding your son, chief, but we go driving into the town square, we are signing our death warrant. We'll be lucky to make it of this vehicle alive."

Gottman slammed the gearstick into reverse and was about to back up when Brody opened the door. "I'm going in. I don't expect you to follow but that could be my son in there."

"Chief!"

"Just go check the radio station. Devan might have gone there."

Michael got out. "I'm going with him."

Gottman slammed his hands against the steering wheel. "Great." Now he felt like a complete dick. Here was an orderly willing to put his neck on the line. What was he meant to do? Drive away? "Ugh. Hold up." He groaned and swung the vehicle into a driveway. Got out, pulled an AR-15 from the back of the trunk and patted the top of his vehicle while nervously looking around. "I'll be back for you."

Brody watched him from the corner treat his car like it had feelings. He shook his head in disbelief and cast a glance down the road. Although he was determined to find Nick, he understood what Gottman was trying to say. An eruption of gunfire, and a Jeep zipping into view made it clear that it wasn't just the infected they might be up against. It was to be expected. Fear of being infected or harmed would throw the nation into a fight-or-flight mentality. It wasn't like those infected were easy to spot until their eyes and skin changed. People only had seconds to determine if someone walking up on them was going to attack or infect them.

They broke into a jog, keeping close to the buildings and staying in a single line with Gottman watching their six. The blackness of night provided much needed cover.

* * *

Sergeant Radcliff bellowed over the radio. "We leave in five minutes, they want us on the roof ready for extraction."

Damian Welch stuck a finger in his ear trying to hear over the sound of gunfire. "What about the kids?"

"No one is to leave."

"But sarge, we don't know if they're infected yet. It's been six hours. If they were infected they would have—"

"No one is to leave, private. That is an order!" he bellowed cutting him off.

"Roger that."

Two weeks a year. That's all, he'd been told. He figured he would do simple shit like being posted at a gate and letting people on and off the base. At the worst he figured he might have to do some time overseas, or handle

border control with the influx of Mexicans. But this…
No, he didn't expect to deal with this. He didn't sign up
to kill Americans, to kill his own kind. He looked over
the group of roughly twenty-five students huddled
together, a mask of fear on their faces. Most had their
hands over their ears, some were crying, others he'd heard
asking for their parents. They were just kids. Not
monsters. They weren't like those outside the walls that
were trying to get in. Insane, lunatics, unable to control
their rage.

"What did the sarge say?" Barett asked.

Welch didn't want to tell him. Barett wouldn't think
twice about putting a slug in one of those kids, he'd been
itching to do it since the attack in the school. If he'd had
his way he would have wiped out all of them.

"Just give me a minute." Welch eyed a black kid who'd
been eyeballing them since they'd arrived, watching their
every move, listening in on their conversations. "You," he
said pointing and gesturing for the kid to meet him across
the room away from the others. The tall, muscular kid got

up and made his way over.

"What's your name, kid?"

"Devan Jones."

Welch looked over at Barett who had gone off to help a couple of the other soldiers hold the tide back from the front entrance. "How old are you?"

"Seventeen."

He nodded. "I have a son a few years younger than you. Look, I'm not going to cherry coat this. I think you know this doesn't end well, right?"

Devan gulped and pursed his lips.

"Although the odds are against you making it out of this alive, if you go out there you stand a better chance of survival. Do I make myself clear?"

The kid nodded.

"I have my orders and I have no choice but to follow them but between now and when I take action, there is a small window of opportunity to leave. But you're going to have to decide if you're ready to take it. You won't get all of these kids out of here. I can't help you with that but I can make sure that emergency exit back there is unlocked. You understand?"

He nodded. Welch jerked his head towards the students to have Devan join them again. He knew he was breaking protocol, and going against a direct order but was he meant to look away as he shot them? How could he ever look his own son in his face and tell him that the nation that he lived in was worth dying for if he had killed his own? Maybe Barett would gladly step over the line but not him.

Welch took a moment to unlock the chain around the emergency exit and cast a glance towards Devan. He was about to head off to inform Barett and the others of the sergeant's instructions when he turned straight into Barett.

"Oh, hey, I was about to come find you."

Barett scowled. "Yeah?" He sidestepped and looked at the door. "Why did you unlock it, Welch?"

There was no easy answer to that, at least none that would satisfy him.

Before he could utter a word, Barett reached for his radio. "Come in, sarge!"

Welch lunged forward tackling him to the ground.

"Devan, now!"

Out the corner of his eye, as he struggled to hold down Barett, he saw the kid and many of the other students race towards the door. A hard fist connected with Welch's face, and they rolled over. Welch hung on for dear life and gritted his teeth. Seeing every kid escape into the night brought more satisfaction than any other point in his career and made every painful blow to his face worth it.

Chapter 27

It was a chaotic scene that played out before them. Nick and the others had taken cover behind a 4 x 4 truck, and were picking off threats in every direction when the door burst open and students scattered.

"Emerick!" Nick said, slapping him on the arm. He turned, and his eyes widened as he too spotted Devan ducking rounds zipping overhead. He went to dash towards him when Chad grabbed his arm.

"Don't be a fool."

"That's my son."

Chad motioned with his head, as students buckled under gunfire. It was hard to tell who was responsible — the military on the roof, or those on the ground. Muzzle flashes had been lighting up the night since they'd run for cover.

Nick lifted his head at the sound of a chopper coming in for landing.

"I can't stand here and do nothing."

Before Emerick or Chad could stop him, Nick darted to the next vehicle, then the next, heading in the direction of Devan. He heard Emerick yelling behind him but couldn't hear exactly what he said. Running with a Glock in his hand, he fired at anyone who came at him. That amounted to two people, a woman holding what looked like a butcher knife, and a young guy gripping a shotgun. There was no time to think, no time for grief or regrets. He acted out of self-preservation, driven by fear of death. The very thing that was devastating the community was keeping him alive. Eventually he made it to a parked Jeep and hopped into the back. Devan was resting behind a tree, looking both ways.

"Devan!" he yelled then waved.

He got this smile on his face as if the cavalry had just arrived. Devan looked to his left and right and then shot out, sprinting the twenty yards to the parked Jeep. Bullets tore into the Jeep, so Devan had to change direction. He made it to a station wagon two vehicles up. Nick waited until the gunfire let up before rolling out of the Jeep, staying low and making his way up to Devan. He let himself into the front, and slammed the door closed just as rounds lanced the windows and sent shards of glass all over them.

"Nick Jackson, you are a sight for sore eyes. I could kiss you right now, my friend."

"Well don't," Nick replied. "Your father is here."

"My father?"

"About fifty yards from here behind a parked 4 x 4."

Another hail of bullets ricocheting off the metal caused them to get low to the floor. "Holy shit. Isn't this something? Could you ever imagine in your wildest—"

"Devan. Shut the hell up."

* * *

Brody had seen his son make a beeline for the station wagon. A wave of relief was quickly followed by fear as he came under heavy gunfire. Unable to pinpoint it he just fired in random directions in the hopes of drawing away the attention from whoever was targeting them.

"Gottman," he yelled. Gottman hurried to the front. "Bring up your vehicle. I've spotted him but we don't have a chance in hell of making it across without some form of cover."

"Lexi isn't a form of cover."

"Dear God, man. Would you stop referring to the damn car as a woman and use some common sense."

"I am. That's why I didn't bring it with me."

A torrent of rounds tore up the earth near them and they pulled back behind the wall. "That's coming from the military on the roof. What the hell are they playing at?"

"They have no idea who we are. Right now everyone is a threat."

Brody turned and looked at Gottman, and Gottman sighed. "All right, I'll get it but if this car gets one scratch..." he trailed off as he sprinted away. Michael pulled up close.

"You know his car is going to get chewed up in the funnel."

"Yep," Brody replied without looking at him.

They watched a Chinook helicopter come in for landing on the roof of the Palace Theater. The rotors whipped furiously sending large wafts of air down.

"That's our distraction," he said turning back and waiting to see headlights. "We get one shot at this."

"Who do you think the ones on the ground are?"

He shrugged. "Infected, gangs, militia. No idea."

He didn't care right now. People had every right to bear arms and protect themselves. Marfa was no longer the quiet little town in the middle of nowhere. It was at the center of what would become a nationwide epidemic. If the military were pulling out, that could only mean one thing. His mind thought of the worst. But he couldn't accept that the government would go that far. Could they?

The familiar sound of the GT's engine roaring caught his attention. The glow of headlights lit up the night as the vehicle tore down the road towards them. Gottman swerved into view, and opened the passenger side. "Get in!"

Both of them hopped in and before he had a chance to close the door Gottman floored it. The smell of tire rubber lingered as the GT took off at a high rate of speed. Almost immediately they came under fire. The back window shattered, and multiple rounds lanced into the side of the vehicle.

"I knew it. I damn well knew it!"

Gottman cursed as the GT bounced up onto the sidewalk and whipped past trees, hitting speeds of up to a hundred. "Hold on!" Gottman yelled as the rear of the car slid out, screeching to a halt just beyond the station wagon. Michael and Brody jumped out and engaged with multiple threats.

"NICK!" Brody bellowed as loud as he could.

"Dad?"

"Go, I'll hold them at bay," Michael said. Brody slid over the front of the GT catching Gottman's narrowed gaze as multiple rounds tore up his vehicle. Oh, he was going to hear about this later.

Brody pulled the door open and clasped his son's hand. "Stay low, and get in the vehicle."

Devan and Nick got out and were about to dart across to the GT when a stream of gunfire tore up the ground beneath them ad pushed them back. The assault was so bad, that Gottman yelled out, "I'm hit!"

Brody took the chance and rushed over and opened his door. Sure enough, a round had penetrated the vehicle and torn through his leg. Brody yanked him out and dragged him to cover. They were pinned down between the GT and the station wagon.

"Michael!" Brody yelled but got no answer.

"Wait here," he said to Nick as he darted to the front of the GT and took a look around. Slumped over and not moving was Michael, his white orderly clothes riddled with round holes that were dark red in color.

Another flurry, and he had no choice but to pull back. Pinned in, unable to move without risking being shot, Brody turned to Nick. "I'm sorry, son."

"For what?"

"Everything. You getting caught in the middle of your mom and I… not acknowledging your pain when Will died, and losing myself in my own."

Nick nodded but didn't respond. Brody didn't expect him to. The wounds were deep in all of them. And now was the time to try and heal. Devan cast a glance over the GT. "They have a high-powered gun on the back of that military Jeep."

"Who are they?" Brody asked.

"Militia is my guess."

"More like maniacs," Nick said. "We need to get to your father."

"Emerick?" Brody asked.

"That's who I've been with this whole time. He's not far from here." Nick pointed in a direction but it was too risky to take a look without getting shot.

Brody did his best to return fire but he was nearly out. "How are you doing for ammo?"

"Not many rounds left," Nick said offering him his gun.

"Keep it. You'll need it."

"On the passenger side is the AR-15," Gottman said, gripping his leg. Brody dashed out and dived into the open car, snatching up the rifle and returning only to find himself spun by a bullet that struck him in the arm. He hit the ground and the rifle slid across close to Devan's feet.

"Dad!" Nick screamed, hurrying over but keeping low.

Devan picked up the AR, glanced at it a few seconds, and unleashed round after round at their attackers. He gazed at it again. "Holy shit. This is the real deal."

"Give me that here, kid," Gottman said.

"Forget it. You can barely hold your leg together," he replied.

Meanwhile Nick pulled his father to safety. He was bleeding badly. "If there was ever a time I needed your mother, it's now."

* * *

Her throat and legs were burning. They hadn't stopped running since leaving Gottman's residence. At night all the streets looked exactly the same — rows of homes, small mom-and-pop stores and now buildings on fire, and vehicles reduced to charred metal. Only minutes earlier, Pete had shot a woman who tried to attack them with an axe. She came out of nowhere, swinging like a madman. The town had fallen into complete disarray, families turning on each other, friends becoming enemies and fear streaking its way through the heart of it all.

Nearby they could hear the sound of a circling chopper overhead trying to locate them. "Come on. Keep going," she yelled.

Jenna wheeled around a corner and dashed out into the road just as a red truck came barreling towards them. She stuck out her arms, and the truck squealed to a halt inches away from her torso.

She came around to the passenger side and begged the two occupants to give them a lift. The driver was hesitant at first but his passenger must have convinced him as he thumbed for them to get in the back. Pete slid in first, followed by her.

"Thanks. I really appreciate it. The name's Jenna, and this is Pete."

The driver turned and gave a wry smile. "Sergio."

Before the passenger could introduce himself a large light shone down on them illuminating the inside of the vehicle. "GO!" she yelled. Sergio's eyes widened but he didn't question why. He slammed his foot against the accelerator and they took off.

"What the hell is going on?"

No sooner had they made it a hundred yards down the main stretch of road than the helicopter cut them off, landing ahead of them. Without knowing what their intentions were, Sergio removed his hands from the wheel and froze as armed military soldiers encircled the truck yelling for them to keep their hands where they could see them. Through the windshield, Jenna saw Colonel Lynch step out of the Chinook.

Her stomach sank.

* * *

Emerick had watched it all play out before him, unable

to do more than return fire. He'd tried to make his way over but had been pushed back by the steady onslaught of gunfire coming from multiple directions. Seeing Brody gave him a glimmer of hope, that was until the GT had been turned to Swiss cheese.

"Chad."

He turned to speak to him but he was gone. Jasper was cowering in the same spot.

"Where did he go?"

"He ran off."

"I knew it. Damn coward. You put your faith in the military and they let you down, over and over again." He shuffled back to cover Jasper when a large dark form off to his right caught his eye. The sound of an engine could be heard, then as the vehicle rolled into a band of moonlight, he saw it was a tan military Humvee.

"Jasper, get in the vehicle. Quick!"

Expecting to encounter resistance, after watching those on the roof shooting the ones below, he was surprised when it jerked to a stop and the door opened and Chad stuck out his head. "Want to get out of here?"

"How the hell did you get that?"

"The perks of being in the military," he said but withholding the full story.

"You bastard. I thought you had left us behind."

"And give up on your pleasantries?" Chad grinned.

They hurried to the side and let themselves in, and Chad veered it in the direction of Devan. Inside Emerick glanced back to see another soldier gripping his stomach.

"Was that you?"

"Who, him? No, that was courtesy of one of our own. No, if it wasn't for him we wouldn't even have this." Emerick didn't have time for the full story. Bullets bounced off the enclosed metal cabin like heavy hail in a storm.

"That's it, bring it up," Emerick said guiding him as he veered up in front of the GT. Emerick brought the window down and yelled to them.

"Get inside."

Their faces lit up.

"They've been hit," Nick yelled.

"Oh shit," he replied noticing the second officer wasn't going to be able to move fast. He hopped out and stayed low using the vehicle as cover while Chad slipped to the back to go up and use the machine gun on top for additional cover. As soon as it kicked in, that was his cue. Emerick darted out and helped his son get the officer into the Humvee, followed by Brody. It took them less than ten seconds, and within twenty they were pulling away from what had become a living hell.

* * *

The Humvee rumbled down the streets, the sound of bullets becoming distant the further they drove south. Nick sat in the back with his hand on his father's wound. Brody smiled at him then glanced at Officer Gottman.

"Where are we heading?" Devan asked

"As far away from this town as possible," Gottman said.

"No, I need to get Jenna," Brody added.

"But that's in Alpine. Twenty-five minutes away,"

Chad said.

"I'm not leaving without my wife."

"I'm afraid you might have to," the wounded soldier curled in the back of the Humvee said. Nick looked his way, as did the rest. "They are going to wipe this town off the map within the hour."

"What?" Brody asked.

"That's why they pulled the troops. This..." he trailed off. "This can't spread more than it already has, and they can't contain it so all that's left is to eliminate it."

"But there are innocent people in this town. Folks who aren't infected."

The soldier looked absently back at him.

"Head to Alpine," Brody said not taking his eyes off the soldier.

"Did you not hear what he said?" Chad replied.

Brody rose from his seat, and leaned forward clasping his military fatigues, and pushing a handgun to his head. "I don't give a fuck. Head to Alpine!" he bellowed. Gottman tried to calm him but he refused to listen. There was no way he was leaving her behind. If this event had shown him anything, it was how much she meant to him, and what really mattered. It wasn't his job, it wasn't the town, and it wasn't even his own pain over the loss of his eldest son. Without her, none of it mattered. And he refused to let twenty-four years flush down the drain.

The Humvee roared as they headed south towards Antonio Street.

Nick looked out the window.

"Nick. You okay?"

He nodded but said nothing, and then suddenly he yelled out. "Stop. Stop the vehicle!"

"What is it now?" Emerick asked. The Humvee came to a crawl and the door opened.

"Callie!" Nick yelled.

Walking down the street, tears rolling down her cheeks and blood caking her face, was Callie Madison. Brody knew her family well. He also knew where they lived and she looked as if she was heading in the opposite direction. Nick hopped out and hurried over to collect her. A moment later she ducked into the Humvee and they continued on their way.

"Callie. Where's Angela?" Emerick asked.

She just shook her head and Emerick's chin dropped.

"Your family. Were they there?" Brody asked.

Callie nodded then began to cry even harder. No one probed her any further, her parents' fate was clear. How it had happened was anyone's guess. As they continued on all Brody could think about now was Jenna.

Her safety was all that mattered.

Chapter 28

His heart was frantic upon arrival at Gottman's home. Although he was suffering from a wound to the arm, Brody was the first out of the Humvee. He raced toward the house screaming her name. "Jenna!"

Silence came back.

He burst through the door and was confronted by the bloody scene in the kitchen. His eyes fell upon the pharmacist, then Sorenson. Neither one was moving. He continued on and saw Liam's body in the living room. Quickly he double-timed it up the stairs and entered the bedroom to find the covers pulled back but Jenna nowhere to be found.

Fear was getting the best of him as he went from room to room.

He hurried down and was met in the hallway by Emerick.

"Brody, we need to go."

"She's not here."

"I'm sorry, man, but if we don't get out of here now—
"

Sorenson started coughing.

"Sorenson?" Brody dropped down to where he was and looked at the knife sticking out of his gut. The knife was still embedded, and he had covered around the wound with pieces of material ripped from his own shirt. By the look of his bloody hands, he'd been applying pressure, trying to let the body form blood clots. Having witnessed enough knife attacks in his time, Brody knew it wasn't uncommon to survive a knife attack if it hadn't hit any main arteries. Still it was dangerous and the chances of living got less the longer it remained untreated. Even if there was not a lot of blood coming out, internal bleeding was the alternative.

"Where is she?"

"I…"

"Jenna. Where is she?" he bellowed.

He was slipping in and out of consciousness and was

no doubt on the brink of death. "Chicago," he mumbled. "They'll take her to the CDC."

"Who?"

"The military."

Brody looked up at Emerick and then rose to his feet.

"We can't take him," Emerick said.

"I didn't say we would."

Brody turned without giving Sorenson another glance. Emerick was the first out the door. Brody was about to leave when Sorenson piped up. "I'm sorry."

Brody stopped walking and looked back at him. He knew he was just a pawn in a game the military was playing, no different than the soldiers. "So am I," Brody said and then darted out, rushing back to the idling Humvee. He hopped in and told Chad where they were heading.

They wasted no time getting out of there. The Humvee tore through the streets and each of them glanced out, taking one final look at the town that would soon be reduced to ash. He looked around at the bruised and battered ragtag group that had been drawn together by the worst situation. It was hard to imagine they would have crossed paths had it not been for fate. As they drove beyond its borders, Brody mumbled under his breath a promise, to himself, to his kid, and to his wife. "I'm coming, Jenna. I'm coming."

* * *

Many hours later, buried in the heart of the Chicago facility of the Centers for Disease Control and Prevention, Colonel Lynch downed a glass of bourbon and stared at an old photo of Major Tim Brown. She'd just got off the phone with his wife and had delivered the bad news. She'd wanted to tell her in person but with the state of the nation, she couldn't. She also didn't want anyone else doing it. She'd met Mia a few times over the years at dinner parties. What Mia didn't know was that Tim had cheated on her a few times. Of course he'd confided in Lynch, as she was the other woman. It was stupid. Both of them knew it, and both had gone into it looking to find something that their own marriages couldn't provide. Intimacy for him, understanding for her. She wasn't proud of it, and they had cut it short before it ruined more than their marriages, but that's why his death stung so badly. He was the only one who really understood the weight that was on her shoulders.

She turned off her cell at the sound of a knock at the door.

"Come in."

Lieutenant Mosley walked in. "They're all prepped."

"Very good."

"How do you wish to proceed?"

"Let's move ahead with the trials, and hope to God that we can find a cure for this before it's too late."

She got up and followed him out, leaving her laptop open with a map of the United States. Six states were marked in red, showing areas where the infection had spread. The president had ordered a cordon sanitaire sealing them off from the rest of the population, troops were sent in to handle the violence, FEMA set up aid camps while medical doctors worked around the clock to find a way to turn back the tide. The military were throwing every resource they had at the problem, and trying their best to protect and ensure the survival of the nation. Easier said than done.

Lynch wasn't a fool.

Even though they had two immunes, that wouldn't solve the problem. Delivery of a vaccine, if they ever created one, would be the challenge. Trust was at an all-time low. And that would only get worse as they sifted through the sick and healthy. There would be many other towns like Marfa and Alpine, others who would fight back and resist, and they would have local militia, neighborhoods and gangs to deal with as nefarious individuals would see opportunity when the country was at its weakest.

Lynch closed the door behind her, confident that she would be the one to turn this around. She would do everything in her power, and that began today. She entered a room which contained a two-way mirror. Beyond it, strapped to two steel tables, dressed in blue scrubs, were Jenna Jackson and Pete Douglas. As doctors began to work, their mouths opened wide but Lynch couldn't hear their screams.

But that didn't matter.

As long as they were immune, there was hope.

This was not the end, just the beginning.

* * *

THANK YOU FOR READING

Unstable: The Amygdala Syndrome book 1. Search on online for book two in January 2019. Please take a second to leave a review, it's really appreciated.

Thanks kindly, Jack.

A Plea

Thank you for reading Unstable: The Amygdala Syndrome book 1. If you enjoyed the book, I would really appreciate it if you would consider leaving a review. Without reviews, an author's books are virtually invisible on the retail sites. It also lets me know what you liked. You can leave a review by visiting the book's page. I would greatly appreciate it. It only takes a couple of seconds.

Thank you — **Jack Hunt**

Newsletter

Thank you for buying Unstable: The Amygdala Syndrome book 1, published by Direct Response Publishing.

Click here to receive special offers, bonus content, and news about new Jack Hunt's books. Sign up for the newsletter. http://www.jackhuntbooks.com/signup/

About the Author

Jack Hunt is the author of horror, sci-fi and post-apocalyptic novels. He currently has three books out in the War Buds Series, Four books out in the EMP Survival series, Two books in the Against all Odds duology, Two books in the Wild Ones series, three in the Camp Zero series, five books out in the Renegades series, three books in the Agora Virus series, and multiple single novels. There is one called Blackout, one called Final Impact, one called Darkest Hour, one called The Year Without Summer, one out in the Armada series, a time travel book called Killing Time and another called Mavericks: Hunters Moon. Jack lives on the East coast of North America.

59705460R00250

Made in the USA
Columbia, SC
06 June 2019